Praise f
CODE BLUE

"Witty, precise, riveting prose... I had important things to do last weekend, important things that I neglected to do because of CODE BLUE. Once I started to read Tom Sigafoos's book, I couldn't put it down."

– Soinbhe Lally,
The Donegal Democrat

"What we want from a detective novel is a set of appropriately sleazy characters – and we get these – and a story which keeps us turning the pages – and we also get this... CODE BLUE is definitely worth a read."

– Dean Baldwin,
Pennsylvania State University

Code Blue

A Frank Chandler Mystery

Tom Sigafoos

Code Blue – A Frank Chandler Mystery
Copyright © Dale Thomas Sigafoos, 2008
Cover: Peacock (detail) by Monica Corish. Used by permission.

The right of Tom Sigafoos to be identified as the Author of the Work has been asserted by him in accordance with the Copyright, Designs, and Patents Act, 1988.

All rights reserved. Apart from any use permitted under Irish, UK, US, and International copyright laws, no part of this publication may be reproduced, stored in a retrieval system, or transmitted, in any form or by any means, without the prior written permission of the author, nor otherwise be circulated in any form of binding or cover other than that in which it is published.

Excerpts from Code Blue may be quoted in reviews.

This is a work of fiction, in whole and in part. Any resemblance of the characters in this novel to actual persons, living or dead, is unintentional and purely coincidental.

ISBN 978-1-4092-3146-2

Published by Lulu.com

To Monica

Author's Note

In a midwest US city in 1977, between jobs but with a little money in the bank, I wrote the first draft of CODE BLUE. In those lightly-computerized days, I copied Raymond Chandler's technique of tearing sheets of legal-sized yellow pads in two and typing a paragraph on each half-page. It worked. Blank 8½-by-11 sheets had loomed in the typewriter carriage like daunting marble slabs, white expanses that did not encourage a hopeful writer to sully them with his words. But the yellow half-pages were friendly and unintimidating, happy to be pecked at and penciled over, cheerfully willing to be wadded up and tossed into the wastebasket if the words took a nose-dive.

I mailed the consolidated manuscript to a dozen publishing houses, leaving the post office each time with the optimistic glow that a fresh lottery ticket produces. A Boston-based publisher kept the manuscript for so long that I wrote to ask if they'd lost it. The Sexy Female Editor of my Dreams wrote back to say that she was circulating it among her colleagues and promoting it for publication, and would I send some biographical information? I sweated over those bio paragraphs longer than over any chapter of CODE BLUE. But a few weeks later the manuscript reappeared in my Self-Addressed Stamped Envelope. Everybody liked it, the Sexy Female Editor wrote, but they just didn't think it would sell.

It's been fun to dust off CODE BLUE after its long repose in a manila folder. I'd forgotten how clunky and traceable typewriters were, even the snazzy electric models. I'm also struck by the number of things which simply weren't around in 1977: cellphones (or "mobiles" here in Ireland), caller ID, call blocking, e-mails, texts, DNA testing, the Internet, and cappuccino. Warning: an appalling number of cigarettes get smoked in this book. How innocent we were.

I hope you enjoy CODE BLUE. It's time for us to shake the mothballs out of our trenchcoats and un-stuff the new generation of stuffed shirts who so desperately deserve it.

Tom Sigafoos
March 2008
County Donegal, Ireland
tomsigafoos@gmail.com

Chapter 1

Siehl wasn't happy. He kept fiddling with a fancy-looking cigarette lighter that sat on his desk. The black plastic base of the thing had been streaked with cream-colored lines to make it look like a block of marble. He'd flicked it six times, and the sparks left a tang of ozone in the air.

I said, "Where did you get that thing?"

"Huh?" He looked at it like he was seeing it for the first time. "This? Hell, I don't know. My secretary gave it to me when I moved here from St. Louis." He flicked it again. "It doesn't work worth shit."

I looked around Siehl's office. He sat at a kidney-shaped desk covered with papers and telephones and dictating equipment. In front of the desk six chairs formed a semicircle around a glass-topped coffee table. There were pictures of redwoods and sand dunes on the walls. It looked like a room where the Nobel Prize Nominating Committee ought to meet. I wondered what Siehl would think of my office.

I said, "The meter is running."

He looked at me like he'd found a cigar butt in the candy dish. "You didn't park on the street, did you?"

"I get a hundred a day, plus expenses. So far you owe me four dollars and seventeen cents."

He scowled and cleared his throat. "Don't you think the first consult ought to be free?"

"Last year I came to this hospital with a broken finger. I don't remember getting any freebies."

He placed the lighter firmly on the desk, like someone who's making a long-deliberated chess move. "How old are you?"

"If that's your idea of a serious question, I can see why you're in trouble."

Siehl bristled, but he didn't say anything. I said, "I imagine that you've got a problem, and you're under some kind of pressure, and you can't trust anybody you know. You probably picked my name out of the phone book. I'll show you my license, but I'll be damned if I'll show you my birth certificate."

Siehl grinned. He wasn't used to being told off, but he didn't mind it. "I thought you'd have steely-gray eyes."

"And?"

"And be at least forty."

"Sounds like you were expecting Nick Charles." I sat perched on the forward edge of the chair seat. Sitting in the middle had been like sinking into a bucket of sawdust. I wondered if Siehl had chosen his low, slouchy furniture with intimidation in mind.

He said, "Have you ever tracked down a poison-pen letter-writer?"

"You're kidding."

"*Bullshit!* What are you grinning at?"

"What are you getting worked up about? Poison-pen letters are sort of quaint. Most people don't get rattled about that kind of crap any more."

He looked sour. "You think this is beneath your dignity?"

"No. I'm just surprised. Have these letters been coming to you?"

"No, not me" He rummaged in the file-drawer of his desk. He stopped and stared into space for a minute, exasperated. He was a youngish thickset man, about thirty-six, with a full neck that was starting to run to fat. He picked up his telephone and dialed a digit. There was a buzz in his outer office, and I heard his secretary say, "Yes?"

"What did I do with that envelope from Ross?"

"You gave it to Barry Alspach, sir."

"Oh, yeah. Thanks." He punched the phone button down with a forefinger and then dialed a four-digit number. "Son of a bitch. I'd lose my nuts if they weren't... Barry! This is Dave. Listen, do you have those letters? Bring them up here, will you. Well, as soon as you can." He hung up and looked at me blankly.

I said, "I can hear your secretary."

"Yeah. Well, it's easier to hear in here than it is out there." He scowled at me. I didn't say anything. He said, "Joanie's really good. She's a Kelly Girl, but

I've kept her for three months." I still didn't say anything. Finally he said, "Look. Would it make you feel any better if I closed the door?"

"I'm wondering why you want a confidential investigation of something that isn't very confidential."

"Well, actually it is. Everybody who knows about it is in Administration, and we're kind of like a family. You know?" I thought about nodding an assent, but I didn't. Siehl said, "Jerry Mosher used to tell me that we ought to put Administration in a separate building about a block away. We could fart around and send memos to each other and not interfere with the hospital." He grinned, with a little effort. More silence hung between us.

I said, "What's being brought up here now?"

"The letters."

"Who's bringing them?"

"Barry Alspach. He's the Administrative Intern."

"Come again?"

Siehl said, "When you get a Master's Degree in Hospital Administration, you have to spend a year working in a hospital. That's an Internship."

"You mean wheeling patients around and working in the labs and that sort of thing?"

"No, in *Administration*." Siehl looked pained. He fished a cigarette out of a shirt pocket and lit it with a throwaway lighter from another pocket. I looked at the black plastic cube. I wished I still smoked.

I said, "Why does Barry Alspach have the

letters?"

"Because I gave them to him. See, he has a Preceptor..." He paused, waiting for me to ask.

"You mean someone like a faculty advisor here on the hospital staff?"

"Yeah. Except that I always think of it as a master-apprentice arrangement. Anyway, Barry has a shitty Preceptor."

"Who's that?"

"George Gibbs. He's the Assistant Administrator." He leaned on *Assistant* just hard enough to make it stick out.

I said, "And you're the Associate Administrator, and you're an echelon higher in the ranks, and you think that you should have been his Preceptor."

"Hell, yes. George Gibbs has been around here for years, and he'll still be an Assistant Administrator when they tear this place down. He looked out the window. He sounded like he could fulminate about George Gibbs for hours.

I said, "Who chooses the Preceptor?"

"Ross does. Ross the Boss."

A tall kid in a brown polyester suit walked into Siehl's outer office. I could hear him ask the secretary if it was okay to come in. He got as far as the doorway and stuck his head through in a gawky way to try to catch Siehl's eye. He was carrying a brown manila envelope. Siehl was still staring out the window. I said, "You have a visitor."

"Oh. Barry! Yeah. Come in. You got the letters?" Barry put the envelope on Siehl's desk. He avoided looking at me directly, and he started edging back toward the door. I could hear his sibilant breathing. Siehl said, "Hey, I want you to meet Frank Chandler. He's going to find out who wrote those letters. This is Barry Alspach."

Relieved at being introduced, Barry stepped over and pumped my hand. "Nice to meet you, Mr. Chandler. Are you a policeman?"

"Sham Shpade."

He didn't seem to get it. He looked at Siehl for help. Siehl said, "Thanks for bringing the stuff up. Did you read any of them?"

"Yes. They're creepy." Barry looked like he'd bitten into something putrid.

Siehl said, "Yeah, there are some really fucked-up people in this world," with the tone of closing the discussion. We all looked at each other for a moment, and then Barry said, "Well, if that takes care of everything..."

"Yeah. Thanks, Barry." We both watched while Barry made his exit. Siehl sighed and said, "He's a good kid, but he needs some Dale Carnegie."

"Or some vocational counseling."

Siehl surprised me by getting mad. "I don't need a lot of smartass remarks!"

"It's nothing personal. Barry just looks like a lamb who's wandered into a barbecue pit. What's in the envelope?"

Siehl muttered, "Jesus Christ," but he opened the envelope anyway. He handed me a thin handful of eight-and-a-half-by-eleven sheets of white paper.

They were xerox copies. One of the copies had a washed-out letterhead of Riverview Hospital at the top. I said, "Where are the originals?"

"Ross has them."

"Does anyone else have copies?"

Siehl stared out the window again. "George Gibbs."

I wondered how many broken legs and appendectomies and cardiac by-pass operations it took each year to pay Siehl and Gibbs and Ross. I looked at the xerox copies. They were neatly typed, without many mistakes or x'ed-out words. The type was ordinary typewriter elite. There were no indentations, paragraphs, salutations, or signatures. Molly Bloom. I picked out the one with the Riverview Hospital letterhead and read it.

> *I suppose you think this is funny, dont you Doctor, you probably think this is a real riot. You think your really putting one over on every body. I think your disgusting, especially when you make Darlene get down on her knees and take it in her mouth and you come all over her face. Or does she like it that way. Ill bet you do, your so old that you cant get it up unless she sucks on it.*

It went on like that for the rest of the page. I glanced through the other letters. They were much the same – mostly oral-sex references, some genital-genital speculations, and a funny three-line digression about pot bellies. There were eight letters in all, including one that rambled on for two pages.

Something in the language kept nibbling at the back of my mind, but it eluded me when I tried to pin it down. I decided to let it swim in the alpha-waves for a while and said, "Who was this addressed to?"

Siehl was lighting another cigarette. "Richard Parker. The Chief of our Medical Staff."

"Who's Darlene?"

Siehl rolled his eyes up to a point about six feet over my head, and then back down. "Darlene Kotecki. She's a Ward Clerk."

"You mean one of those little honeys in a pink smock that all the nurses boss around?"

"Yeah," he said unenthusiastically. "Richard Parker's old enough to be her father. He could damn near be her grandfather." He scowled at me, trying to get into some sort of hospital-administrator attitude. "You haven't read all of those already, have you?"

"Only enough to wonder why anybody gives a rat's ass about the whole business. Doctors get weird mail every day."

He sulked and said, "It's different in a hospital."

I said, "When I worked in a hospital, people screwed each other the same way they do in insurance companies and police departments and everyplace else. The only difference here is that your Chief of Staff is breaking the code." Siehl was sitting bolt upright, scowling hard, but listening. I said, "It's okay for doctors to screw nurses, because they make enough money to know which fork to use, and a lot of them went into nursing to hook up with a doctor anyway. But Ward Clerks are too many rungs down the ladder. It's sort of like screwing the girls from Housekeeping down in the mop closet."

"Well..."

"So your Doctor Parker is getting a little on the side from Darlene. I assume he's married..."

Siehl nodded.

"...and he's not only breaking the rules and making an ass of himself, but somebody has the indelicacy to send him letters that say what everybody's thinking, more or less. He gets scared, because it's obviously an unpredictable creep who might call his wife some day. Besides that, his pride is hurt. So he leans on the Administrator to do something about it..."

Siehl nodded again.

"...and the Administrator makes copies of these two-bit attempts at pornography and gives them to his Associate Administrator and his Assistant Administrator. Now it's a horse-race to see who can bring in the doctor's pen pal and teach him how to use apostrophes."

"Or her," Siehl said.

"I wasn't leaving anybody out. *Him* includes *her* in this case."

"I want you to come over some night and explain that to my wife." He grinned. We were getting to be friends again.

I said, "I don't see any extortion here. It's just

petty harassment. Why don't you turn the whole mess over to Security?"

Siehl's sunny disposition began to fade. "Our Security Director couldn't find his butt with both hands."

"Who does he work for?"

"George Gibbs."

We sat for a while and listened to the heating system run. Outside it was cloudy. It still had two weeks to snow before Christmas. A wing of the hospital was visible through Siehl's window. A woman in a lime-green bathrobe stood in one of the rooms. She stood awkwardly, as though her stomach hurt.

Siehl said, "I know who's doing it."

I waited until he looked at me before I said, "Who?"

"Joyce Gruber. She's a Head Nurse, and she used to screw Richard Parker." He stared at me again. I didn't like the fervor in the stare. "Think you could check her out?"

"I'm not going to put anybody's fingerprints on the typewriter."

"Just check her out. I've got a great cover-story worked out for you." I didn't say anything. He said. "I'll introduce you around and tell the staff that you're going to do an attitude survey. Then you can talk to anybody."

"What's an attitude survey?"

"Here, I'll show you." He reached into his credenza and handed me a vinyl binder with some fancy printing on the cover.

RIVERVIEW HOSPITAL
EMPLOYEE ATTITUDE SURVEY.
T.A. CARNEY MANAGEMENT CONSULTANTS

Inside there was a table of contents – *Management, Policies, Facilities*, and other headings. After the first few pages, everything was in quotation marks. *"I feel that there's a real communications problem with the Administration."* And so forth.

I said, "Your employees said this?" Siehl nodded. I said, "You paid somebody to listen to all of this stuff and write it down?"

"It wasn't just somebody. T.A. Carney's one of the biggest consulting firms in the country."

"And this is supposed to reflect everybody's unvarnished opinion?"

"All the surveys were confidential." He said it a little too fast, like an over-rehearsed actor.

"If I worked here, I'd have a hell of a hard time believing that."

He squirmed for a minute, but it was because he was itching to tell me something. He said, "I guess if you're going to play the role, you ought to know. You're right. For an extra three thousand dollars, we got a copy of the survey with all of the people identified."

I said, "I'll be a son of a bitch," and I stood up and walked over to the window. The woman in the green bathrobe had gone. Back to bed, I hoped.

Siehl stood up. He didn't know what to do. I walked back over to the chair and sat down, and so did he. I said, "I don't use cover stories, but I'm going to remember that one."

"Why?"

"I'm going to keep it in mind the next time somebody accuses me of making a dirty dollar."

We sat there for a while. The secretary typed in the outer office. I wondered how many days I could poke around Riverview Hospital before somebody threw a fit. Not many. I said, "I'll look for your letter writer. I'll need a five hundred dollar retainer."

Siehl said *Jesus* softly, but he pulled a checkbook out of his suitcoat pocket. He wrote out a check and handed it to me.

I said, "This is a personal check."

He bristled again. "Yeah, it's personal. It's good."

"That's not the point. If I'm working for you and not for the hospital, then I've got no right to be here unless I've got a sick friend. If I start asking questions and somebody gets irritated, they can have me thrown out with every justification in the book. Does Ross know about this?"

"Ross," said Siehl, "doesn't know shit from apple-butter. I'll take care of him. And I'll take care of anybody else who complains. For Christ's sake, I've already told you who to check out. What the hell more do you want?"

"Just a reasonable chance at finding the truth. But you're paying the freight." He glowered at me, but he kept quiet. I said, "I'll need to see some

Personnel files. Darlene Kotecki's, Joyce Gruber's, and Richard Parker's."

"We don't keep Personnel files on the doctors." He dialed his phone, and we stared at each other with blank expressions while it rang somewhere. I could hear and half-see his secretary putting a vinyl cover over her typewriter. Siehl finally hung up. He said, "Those bastards down in Personnel all go home at five o'clock," and he reached for another cigarette.

"I imagine that's what they're getting paid for. I can see the files tomorrow. Is there any place where I can get a look at these people tonight?"

"Parker takes Darlene over to the bar at the Vickers Hotel pretty often."

Siehl was winding down. He looked tired and miserable. I put the xeroxed letters back in the brown envelope, picked up my coat, and stood up. I didn't want to leave him looking like he'd lost his last friend. I said, "Who was the guy who told you to move your office out into the cow pasture?"

"You mean Jerry Mosher? He used to work here. He was a Systems Analyst, and he was the only one who ever got the payroll to run right. Really a bright guy."

"Isn't he here any more?"

"No. Ross fired him. He wanted Jerry to work up a computerized index for all of our memos and correspondence and shit. Jerry told him that it'd be a waste of time, and Ross fired him for insubordination. Dumb bastard."

"Where is he now?"

Siehl grinned and shook his head. "He wangled a grant from the University of Michigan to study superstitions. He's down in the Virgin Islands or someplace."

"Sounds like more fun than payroll," I said. "Here's my card. Do you have an extension here that doesn't go through the switchboard?"

Siehl dug a business card out of his desk and scribbled a number on the back. I was on my way out the door when he said, "Hey! Who's Nick Charles?"

"Don't you ever go to the movies?"

"Christ, I don't have time to do anything any more." He was reaching for the phone again when I left.

In the outer office Siehl's secretary was putting on a winter coat. I stepped behind her and helped her slip her arm through the sleeve. She smiled a gorgeous smile and said, "Thank you."

"If you smile like that again, I'll help you put on most anything."

"You ought to come around here more often. You just made my day." She was wearing a white turtleneck sweater and skirt, and she carried her head high. She looked smashing. She also had a wedding ring on her hand.

From inside his office Siehl hollered, "Joanie?" She shrugged and turned toward his door. I said, "I'll be seeing you," and stepped out into the hall.

I walked past doors labelled *Assistant Administrator*, *Communications*, and *Security*. The hall carpet was a yellow-orange indoor-outdoor type that flowed into all of the offices. The walls were covered with a rough textured twine-colored material, and there were more Sierra Club photographs hanging between the doors. It looked like a model home that nobody would ever live in.

Barry Alspach stepped out of a stairwell doorway at the end of the hall. He was carrying the kind of briefcase that studious kids carry, a fat vinyl-covered thing that was big enough to hold a car battery. Barry stood crookedly, as though he was lugging half a set of encyclopedias. I said, "Hello."

"Hello, Mr. Chandler." He looked like he didn't know whether to wait for me to pass or to fall into step with me. I stopped and watched while he shifted the briefcase from one hand to the other.

I said, "You stealing the sash weights?"

He blinked uncertainly. "What's a sash weight?"

"Barry, you make me feel like I'm a hundred years old. What do you have in that thing?"

"Oh, just some of the projects that I've been working on." He lowered the briefcase to the floor and wheezed.

"Do you always take that much work home?"

He grinned, half-pleased and half-embarrassed. "I guess so. Yes, I do. I don't know how people keep up if they don't."

"I think the trick is not worrying about keeping up. But you look to me like the kind of guy who works hard and carries the load for six other people."

"You know, I feel that way sometimes." He looked at the brown manila envelope I was carrying.

"How are you going to look for..." I didn't say anything. He looked at me and tried again. "How can you tell who wrote something like that?"

I liked him. He wasn't too sure of himself, but he wasn't afraid, either. I said, "I don't know. If it's a crazy person, it could be anybody. If it's somebody who's doing it maliciously, then there's a reason involved. I don't know enough about the people or circumstances yet to make any guesses about the reasons. You could probably figure it out faster than I can right now."

Barry said, "You know, that sounds like *A Challenge to the Reader.* I never could get those."

"You were being flim-flammed there. In real life you have to figure out why anybody would bother to pull a lot of the crap that goes on. Their motives are usually so petty that it's surprising."

"You mean like Watergate?"

"Exactly."

Barry looked ruefully at his overloaded briefcase. "I'm going to have a hard time concentrating tonight."

I said, "Let's make a deal. If you can figure this out before I do, I'll split my fee with you."

"Really?"

"Hell, yes. This is a penny-ante job. You already know everybody who's involved. And you look like you could stand a change from reading floor plans, or whatever it is that you're doing. Why don't you think about it?"

He was beaming. "Okay, Mr. Chandler.

Thanks." He picked up his briefcase. "I just wish I knew where to start."

"Drink a few beers and free-think it. *Malt does more than Milton can...*"

He got that insecure expression again. "You know, I don't understand what you're saying half the time."

"It's partly intentional. See you around, Barry."

He headed down the hall in the direction that I'd come from. I stepped through a set of double doors and into the lobby. The place was filling with people who had come to visit the sick ones upstairs. There was a low hubbub of conversation and occasional giddy laughter, but the undertone was anxious. A hospital was no place where anyone wanted to be. Two women in gray uniforms dispensed visitors' passes from behind a desk covered with file-boxes. A sign behind them said *Children Under 14 Are Not Permitted Beyond the Lobby or the Coffee Shop.* The rest of us weren't that lucky.

Chapter 2

The bar in the Vickers Hotel was as dark as Blanche DuBois's sitting-room. There were heavy velvet drapes and lots of walnut woodwork to keep it that way. Four women and two men were sitting on stools around a piano bar, stumbling through the lyrics of "The Nightingales Sang in Berkeley Square." They were all about Noel Coward's age. Two young black guys in three-piece suits were sitting at the other bar, solemnly attentive to each other's conversation. A uniformed bartender was watching a situation-comedy rerun on a six-inch television, and a waitress who was about the same age as the piano-bar choir was smoking a cigarette.

    I took a seat at the bar where I could see Parker and Darlene in the mirror behind the liquor shelf. It had to be them. They were sitting at a table as far away from the door as possible, beside a wall that had been decorated to look like natural rock with ferns and mosses. The lights that shined on the rock-wall also highlighted Darlene's hair. She was a small girl, but she had a huge white-blonde mane. Her face looked tiny. She sat up straight, not leaning back, with her mouth fixed in a tense half-smile that didn't include her eyes. Richard Parker sat close to her, leaning over her with his arm stretched around the back of her chair. He had been handsome, but he was getting jowls. He looked like a Roman Senator. She looked like a cashier in a discount store.

I ordered a scotch-and-water and thought about the letters in the brown manila envelope in the glove compartment of my car. I wondered if Parker really gave a damn about the letters, or if he'd simply popped off at Ross in a fit of pique. I wondered if he was trying to protect himself or Darlene or his wife. I wondered if I'd be chasing thin young girls when I turned fifty-five.

Parker signaled for two more drinks by pointing his finger at the empty glasses on their table, and the waitress said, "Yes, Doctor," in a mechanical tone. Darlene said something to Parker, and she slid out of her chair. She walked toward the ladies' room with her shoulders hunched over in a miasma of self-consciousness. The waitress glanced at her with eyes as expressionless as the bottoms of the bar glasses. I walked over to the table. "Doctor Parker?"

His head snapped up; he'd been lost in thought. "Yes?"

"My name is Frank Chandler. I've been hired to find the person who's been writing poison-pen letters to you."

He drew himself up in his seat. He was a big man, bigger than he'd seemed when he was curled around Darlene. "And who has hired you to do this thing?"

"David Siehl."

He looked down at his drink. "Well, I'll be goddamned. Sit down." It was more of an instruction than an invitation, but I sat down anyway. He said, "Why are you telling me this?"

He was giving me his best professional you'd-better-tell-the-truth stare, and he was good at it. I said, "I'm telling you because otherwise I can't work. I usually get hired by people who are in trouble, not by third parties. Things could get damned complicated if you didn't know whose side I was on. You might even get the idea that I was tailing you and reporting back to your wife."

Parker sneered at me. "And now I'm to believe that you're telling the absolute truth?"

"You don't have to believe me. Call Siehl and check it out. But for now I can tell you that I've seen the letters. Since one of them is written on Riverview Hospital stationery, it's probably a Riverview employee, and that's where I'm going to start looking. But you're the Chief of Staff, and you have the authority to get me thrown out on my ear. It'd be a shame if I found out who it was and then couldn't get in to tell you about it."

"You're a cocky son of a bitch, you know that?"

"If you want some humble types to work on

your investigation, I'll get them for you. They'll still be analyzing the glue on the stamps when this character starts calling you at home."

Parker looked down at his drink again. "She already has."

"Oh? Since when?"

"For about two weeks now. My wife..." He trailed off.

"Is there any conversation?"

"No. There's no sound at all. It's like a broken connection,

"Sometimes they'll unscrew the mouthpiece off the phone." Parker was in a reverie. I wondered what kind of doctor he was. I said, "Why did you say she?"

He held his swizzle-stick like a pencil and poked at the tablecloth with it. He said, "This has happened to me before, you know."

"Recently?"

"No, it was ten years ago. In Philadelphia. I became involved with a Social Worker at the hospital..." He cut off his sentence and looked at me apprehensively.

I said, "Yes," trying not to look like a hanging judge.

"...and when I stopped seeing her, she started writing to me and calling me at home. She even sat in her car across the street from my house. For hours."

"Do you think that she's involved in this business now?"

"No," Parker said. "She's married and living in Denver." He stared off into space.

"Are you absolutely sure? If she did it before, she's the prime candidate..."

"Please don't insult my intelligence, Chandler. I'm sure that she's not involved." He set his jaw and looked around the room for Darlene, who was nowhere in sight. I tried to imagine Parker getting excited enough to put pressure on a hospital administrator. He looked like he was half asleep. I wondered how he acted when he got mad.

I said, "How long have you been getting the letters?"

"Since October."

"Who do you believe is sending them?"

He cocked an eyebrow at me. "That is what I expect you're being paid to find out."

"Right. I'm being paid. I get paid to sit in stuffy bars with middle-aged men who're trying to prove they can still charm the pants off the hired help."

Parker got beet red. "Let me see your license, you son of a bitch."

"You show me yours and I'll show you mine."

"If I catch you in my hospital I'll have you arrested."

"You do that. And when your ex-girlfriend starts parking her car in your driveway, you can have her arrested, too."

He winced and began to rub his temples. The bartender and waitress were discreetly craning to hear us yell at each other again. Parker looked old and tired. I said, "Doctor, whoever is writing those letters is sick. She's going to get crazier if we don't find her and get her some help. Do you have any idea who it is?"

Parker stared sadly at the table. "Last year I became involved with a nurse named Joyce Gruber. I've suspected that it's her."

"Why don't you take her to lunch and ask her?"

Parker had stopped listening. He was staring over my shoulder, ignoring me. I craned around to see Darlene on her way back from the bathroom. Parker waited until she was six feet away from the table, and then he leaned over and whispered, "I'm sure it's Joyce. You nail her."

He stood up decorously and pulled out Darlene's chair. I stood up, too. He said, "This is Mr. Chandler, dear." He had a bit of the grand manner in his voice. Doctor Parker, in control.

Darlene said, "Hello, sir," and sat down. Parker said, "I'll be very interested to see what you find, Chandler," in a tone that you'd use to dismiss the butler, and he sat down, too.

I looked at the two of them sitting in the defiant glow of their adultery. But they weren't paying the freight. I said, "Don't worry, Doctor. I'll nail the guilty party, even if it's your wife." Parker glared at me like he was going to have apoplexy. I said, "Pleased to meet you, Miss Kotecki," ignored the remains of my drink, and left.

To hell with them. To hell with all of them.

Wet leaves lined the streets of Eden Park, and the pavement felt slippery on the curves. The sun was down, but there was an intense orange-yellow-purple sunset hanging above the horizon. I passed a group of students from the Art Academy with sketch-pads and tackle-boxes, dressed in a rag-bag collection of old Army jackets and second-hand overcoats, waiting in the shelter for a bus. The sunset appeared in glimpses and flashes between the houses as I drove into the Mount Adams district. I crossed the Ida Street viaduct, parked the Fairlane, and walked back to the middle of the bridge.

The sunset still had a gorgeous red-and-violet sheen. From the bridge it silhouetted the downtown buildings and the hills that surrounded the central-city basin. It was a good-looking city, a city that had a reason for being where she was and doing what she was doing. I used to think of her as a nervous old dowager who'd look for any excuse to call the police. Now she seemed more like a parson's widow, ready to kick up her heels a little.

There was a brisk wind, and I turned up my collar and stamped my feet. *Nail her. Check her out.* I'd worked for people that I liked a lot less than Parker and Siehl. What I hadn't seen before was the flurry of interest in sad, twisted little love-notes like the ones in the car. Was it an elaborate set-up? I chewed over the idea for a while, but I couldn't imagine who'd benefit from it. They'd both tried to steer me toward Joyce Gruber, but Parker had mentioned her only after I'd leaned on him. If they were playing games, they were damned good at it.

I walked back to the car and drove the last three

blocks to my apartment building. I had to park a block away, and I swore for the hundredth time that my next apartment was going to have a garage. There was a phone bill in the mailbox and a postcard from my dentist reminding me that it had been a year since I'd had my teeth drilled. I let myself in, put the brown manila envelope on the kitchen table, and got a beer out of the refrigerator. I checked the phone-answering gadget for recorded messages. Nothing.

I rummaged through the kitchen cupboards and the vegetable bin. There were enough odds and ends to make a curry. While I chopped and mixed and browned things, my irritation about Parker and Siehl went away. I had another beer while the curry was simmering. I decided to eat it straight, without rice. I didn't want to feel guilty while I watched a pot of uneaten rice grow moldy in the refrigerator for a week.

After dinner I spread the letters out on the kitchen table and read them all from beginning to end. I opened another beer and took a long pull on it. The sex was just sex, and whoever wrote the letters had so little imagination that it sounded about as exciting as taking a bath. The offensive part was the whining tone that said *You'd better feel sorry because I feel so bad.* Not with a bang but a whimper.

I looked out the window at the lights of Kentucky across the river valley. Parker was a doctor. He was no spring chicken. He must have confronted a lot of people who had raged and cried when he screwed up their treatment. He had to have misdiagnosed a few, and maybe even killed some. And he must have found ways of handling it personally. But now he got upset about snivelling letters from an ex-girlfriend. Why?

I got the gooseneck lamp out of the closet and set it up on the kitchen table. The xeroxes were good copies, but they were blurry under close scrutiny. They had all been done on the same typewriter. The lower-case w's and i's were higher than the other letters, and the n's were lower. I knew that there were other, more definitive characteristics that the police lab could pick out under a microscope, but I could see enough to work with. If I got caught running around with a magnifying glass, I'd never live it down.

I tore off half of one of the letters, folded it, and stuck it in my wallet. I put the others back in the envelope and looked at the mess of dishes and tin cans I'd made in the kitchen. It was eight-thirty. I wondered if Parker and Darlene were shacked up somewhere. The more I thought about Parker, the less I liked him. If he wanted to screw sad, mousy Ward Clerks, that was his business. But I hadn't liked his eagerness to sweep Joyce Gruber out of his life. I wondered if he took showers right after he had sex.

I took Siehl's check out of my wallet and looked at it. I could give it back to him and tell him to spend it on a good psychiatrist for his Chief of Staff. He'd probably hire a surveillance freak instead. I realized that I didn't like Siehl any better than Parker. I wondered if he was at home hassling with a family or hiding out in the gloom of a bar.

I didn't like most of the people who could afford to hire me. By the time I'd fetched home their runaway children, I was usually convinced that the kids were better off where I'd found them. By the time I'd fingered their embezzlers and pilferers, I was sure that they wouldn't screw around if they got paid a decent salary. Siehl and Parker were just two more aging boys who were trying to grow up. But their money would buy as many pounds of potatoes as anybody else's.

I turned my conscience to *low* and looked up Parker's number in the phone book. He was in both the yellow pages and the white pages, and a separate number was listed under *Children's Residence*.

I found *Gruber J* listed on Dixsmyth Avenue, and I wrote down her address and phone number. There was no Darlene Kotecki in the book. I called Information and asked for her number. The operator put a suspicious tone into her voice and told me that Darlene was unlisted.

I took the brown manila envelope into the bedroom and locked it in the desk. I sat and drummed my fingers for a while. It could turn into a bad night if I didn't find something else to do. There were six new paperbacks, still in the bag they came in, sitting on the bookshelf. I fished out *The Book of Daniel* by Doctorow, went back into the living room, and stretched out to read in the brown leather chair.

At eleven-thirty the phone rang. I picked it up and said, "Hello," but there was no response. I waited about ten seconds and said, "Hello," again. Nobody said anything, but the phone wasn't dead. I could hear a hollow, asthmatic breathing that was almost fast enough to be panting. It didn't sound like a thirteen-year-old girl fooling around at a slumber party, but it didn't sound like a threat, either. I said, "You don't have to talk now if you don't want to. I'll be here all night..." There was a click, and the line went dead.

I sat by the phone for the next fifteen minutes, but it didn't ring again. I drank more beer and paced around and read fitfully at Doctorow. At 1:30 I unplugged the phone from the living-room jack and reconnected it in the bedroom. I told myself twenty times that it was only a schmuck who liked to call random numbers at night. But I didn't believe it, and I couldn't get to sleep for a long time.

Chapter 3

The next morning I put on sweatpants and three sweatshirts and a watch-cap to go running. There was a glaze of frost on the trees and grass in Eden Park. Two cars were parked by the Playhouse Circle overlook, and the man and the woman who had driven them were necking in one of the cars. They were there four times a week. I always wondered if they were smooching before going to the office or having a rendezvous on the way home from the night shift. There just never seemed to be a chance to ask.

I showered and dressed and ate bacon and eggs. I brought the telephone back into the living room and hooked it up to the answering machine. I wished that I'd made a recording of the midnight call. Maybe if the caller had heard my authoritarian tones on the machine, he'd have left his name and phone number. I hurried through a second cup of coffee, scanned the morning paper, and thought about Siehl and Parker again. Their intrigues seemed even more trivial by daylight.

I drove to the bank and deposited Siehl's check at the drive-in window. I got to Riverview Hospital at nine-thirty. There was no brass band to welcome me to the lobby, but there wasn't a Security Guard, either. An old black man in a baggy brown Housekeeping uniform was emptying ashtrays. I walked through the swinging doors and into the cool corridor of the Administration suite.

Joan was typing when I came in. She looked up and said, "Hi," while her fingers were still moving. She finished the sentence, looked back at her typewriter, and said, "Oh, shit!"

I said, "Aay, ess, dee, eff, gee..."

"I know what it is, smarty." She stuck a piece of flimsy yellow paper over the last word she'd typed and pecked at a letter to hide her mistake. She pulled out the paper and blew away a little cloud of white dust.

I said, "Is that your request for a raise?"

"No, it's a job description for a file clerk. Are you interested?" She pulled the paper out of the typewriter and inspected it with mock seriousness. "I'm sure that you're qualified."

I diddled with the pencils in a brass cup on the desk. "I'd be interested in a good Executive Secretary, if I could find one."

She leaned back in her chair and looked me over like an oil painting at a dime store. "I'd be interested in a good comedian, if I could find one."

"We can't let this go to waste. I'll get us a club date in Las Vegas."

"That's what they all say."

"Who's they?"

"All the detectives who come in here."

She was laughing with her eyes, but the rest of her face was a near-perfect dead pan. I tried to match it, but I started to grin. "Oh, hell. Let's get out of here and get a cup of coffee."

"Mmm-hmm. First it's Las Vegas, and now it's coffee."

"I'll bet you've got gorgeous dimples on your back."

She tried to look mysterious, but it slipped. "Dimples? On my back?"

"Sure. Haven't you ever looked?"

She touched her fingertips together and shook her head in exaggerated disbelief. Her wedding ring had a fair-sized diamond on it. She said, "I've never met a dimple man before. I'll bet you get a special magazine and everything."

"Yeah, but we have to trade off with the belly-button people every other month." That ring kept glinting at me. "Where's Siehl?"

"Oh, he's in a meeting. I wish you wouldn't get serious, though."

"Why?"

"Because if you leave, I'm going to have to sit here and type for the rest of the morning. After a while I begin to get squirrelly."

"God, yes. If I had to do that, I'd go nuts in an

hour. Why do you do it if you don't like it?"

She stepped back within herself a notch. "That's a long story. Why do you do what you do?"

"Do you know what I do?"

"Yes, and, as a matter of fact, I was envying you yesterday."

"Why?"

"I wasn't eavesdropping, but I can hear everything that goes on in Mr. Siehl's office. You have a really interesting problem to work on, for one thing. And you're not all tied-up and tripping-over-yourself like most people are." I didn't say anything. It would have been a terrible time to stutter or burp. She said, "I was thinking while I drove home last night that it would be fun to track somebody down like a detective. But then I began to imagine what it would be like to actually catch somebody and turn them in, and I didn't think I could do that. I'd think of them more as people than as criminals. Do you know what I mean?"

"Lady," I said, "you don't know the half of it."

"You do it even though it bothers you?"

I said, "It's inside work. No heavy lifting. Did Siehl get those Personnel files for me?"

"I got them for you." She handed me a white plastic file-folder labeled GRUBER, JOYCE M., R.N. Joyce's picture was stapled to an application form inside the folder. She had high cheekbones and a go-to-hell mouth. Her eyes looked tired.

I said, "Where's Darlene Kotecki's?"

"It wasn't there. The Security people had

already taken it out."

"How do you know that?"

"I talked to the girls in Personnel. They get as bored and monotonous as I do. I mean their *work* is monotonous... Anyway, when I couldn't find Darlene's file, I asked Louise, the old lady down there, and she told me all kinds of things. She said that Security goes down there all the time to pull files on girls that the doctors and administrators want to go out with. I let her think that Mr. Siehl wanted Joyce Gruber's file for the same reason."

"What were you going to tell her otherwise?"

"Oh, I was going to say that Joyce was being considered for Employee of the Month."

I was beginning to hope that the wedding ring was a ruse. I said, "Why in the world are you wasting your time as a secretary?"

She hesitated for a second, and then she put on a mock-innocent face and batted her eyelashes like Vivian Leigh. "Ah'm just waiting for someone to come along and take me away from all this."

I pulled my upper lip down over my teeth and said, "Shweetheart, why don't you get a private license? Go into business with me. With your brains and my charm we can't miss."

"Is this where I'm supposed to say *Here's looking at you, kid?*"

A balding, pear-shaped man in an off-the-rack suit bustled in from the hall. He moved with jerky steps and gestures, like a police buff who's been sent out to get the coffee. He said to Joan, "Have you seen

Barry?"

"No, Mr. Gibbs."

"Well, where is he?" He looked over his shoulder at me as though he expected me to leave.

Joan said, "I haven't seen him all morning, sir."

"Well. Mr. Ross wants him at the Administrative meeting."

"I'll try to call him at home, sir."

He said, "My secretary's already tried. I thought that Dave might have sent him on one of his wild-goose-chases."

I said, "Maybe he's up on the floors learning about the hospital."

Gibbs looked indignant. When he got older he was going to look like Lester Maddox. He said, "And who are you?"

"I'm doing an attitude survey."

He whipped around to Joan. "Is this another one of Dave's ideas?" She didn't say anything. He started to build up more steam, but he remembered what he came in for. "Well, if you find out where Barry is, tell him to come to my office right away. The Administrative meeting starts in five minutes." He bustled out the same way he'd bustled in.

Joan started dialing the phone said, "I think I'll try to call Barry anyway," when it hit me. "What's the matter?"

"Does Barry have asthma?"

"I don't know. Why?"

"Where's his office?"

"It's upstairs from here. I think it's 216. You

take the stairs..."

I was halfway down the hall. I could mend fences with Joan later. There was a green EXIT sign that pointed to a stairwell. I went up the stairs two at a time. The second-floor corridor had a smooth floor like the lobby. It must have been a hall of patient rooms at one time. Now it housed a row of cramped one-room offices with cheap plastic name-plates on the doors. *Social Services. Credit and Collections. B. Alspach, Administrative Intern.*

The door wasn't locked. Barry's office was stuffy from overnight heat. Nobody was there. I walked around to his desk and looked in the top center drawer, the wide flat one where people keep their life savers and matches and personal paraphernalia. There was an inhaler in Barry's drawer, the L-shaped kind with a small bottle of compressed antihistamine gas and a round mouthpiece.

I hurried back down to Siehl's office. Joan was typing again. She looked up at me more guardedly than before. She said, "Is this the charm you were telling me about?"

I said, "Later. Where does Barry live?"

"Somewhere over in Clifton, I think." She dialed a four-digit number on her phone. "Louise? This is Joan again. Mr. Siehl needs to know Barry Alspach"s home address. Yes, I'll wait." She cupped her hand over the mouthpiece and looked up at me. "Why are you worried about Barry?"

"It's probably nothing. I hope it is."

"You won't tell me?"

"If I'm wrong, I'll tell you. If I'm right, I won't have to."

She made a mouth that showed how little she thought of my conversation. She said, "Yes, Louise...That's 427 Probasco, Apartment G. Thank you." I said, "Thanks," and headed out the door.

Clifton was the University district, and Probasco Street ran sharply downhill from the campus. Barry's address was a squatty-looking brick apartment house with four units in the front and four more in the back. It looked like it had been built in the Twenties. It was the kind of building where no female tenant in her right mind would use the washer and dryer in the basement.

The row of built-in mailboxes in the closet-sized foyer was covered with a blur of old tenants' names, scrawled messages, odds and ends of scotch tape, and the inevitable *Fuck You* done with a ballpoint. Barry had put his name on his mailbox with a plastic strip from a Dymo marker. I pushed the doorbell under his mailbox, but it wouldn't budge. It looked like it had been varnished over. I tried the inside door, and it wasn't locked.

His apartment was upstairs and at the back. I knocked and listened. A barely-audible Joni Mitchell song drifted up from a downstairs apartment. Even if the place was old and neglected, it was solidly built. Nobody came to the door.

Barry could have stayed all night with a

girlfriend and overslept. He could have gone to the podiatrist to have his bunions pared. He could have decided that Riverview Hospital could run on its own steam today, rolled three joints, and headed for the park. I could do the same. Instead I took the plastic strip out of my wallet and slipped it behind the tongue on the door-lock. The door was so loose you could practically reach it with a finger. I let myself in and closed the door softly.

The apartment was furnished with Salvation Army leftovers. The couch, chair and end table were strictly Ma and Pa Kettle, but the lamps were expensive-looking and contemporary. There were framed Miro and Modigliani prints on the wall. They looked awful on the cheesy wallpaper. I guessed that Barry had taken the place as a low-budget cubbyhole until he could afford snazzy digs with a balcony and a Swedish fireplace. There was a desk covered with a clutter of back issues of *Hospitals* magazine, a volume of *Hospital Administration* by McEacheran, and a typewriter. There were two empty beer bottles on the desk. The briefcase was on the floor, unopened.

I walked as quietly as possible to the bedroom. The single bed must have come with the apartment. It was made up and tucked in so carefully that an old maid could have slept in it. I opened the door to the closet. It was full of expensive new suits. A dresser with peeling veneer held three drawers of shirts in their laundry-wrappers. There was a portrait photograph on the dresser. A rugged-looking man and a tense-looking woman were staring intently at something to the left of the frame.

The phone was on a table by the head of the bed. The phone book was on the floor, open to the "C" section. I flopped it shut with my foot. I wanted to leave and never come back.

I opened the door to the bathroom and found Barry sprawled on the floor beside the tub. He must have tried to crawl out at the last minute before his strength slipped completely away. Both of his wrists were slashed, and the tub was full of bloody water. I crouched down and touched the carotid artery in his neck. He was stone cold and rigid. There wasn't a hint of a heartbeat.

I stepped back and closed the bathroom door. I went into the living room and sat down at the desk. There was a yellow pad covered with scribbled notes. I tore off the top sheet, flipped it over, and stuck it in the typewriter. I typed *The quick brown fox jumps over the lazy dog* three times and made a hell of a clatter. I pulled the paper out and stuck it in an inside suitcoat pocket. Then I took out a handkerchief and rubbed all of the typewriter keys.

The phone rang and I jumped six feet. I let myself out of the apartment and heard the lock snick shut. The hall was still as quiet as the attic of a nunnery. I went back downstairs and outside, trying not to look like I'd just escaped from Leavenworth. I walked up the street and around the corner to where I'd left the car.

I drove to a restaurant five blocks away. There was a telephone booth across the street. There were two broken panes of glass in the door, and someone had stolen the phone book. I dialed the Police Department, and they picked up on the third ring. "Downtown, Sergeant Mason."

"There's been a suicide at 427 Probasco, Apartment G." The sergeant said, "Who is this calling?" and I hung up. I walked back over to the restaurant. It was a plasticky franchised place that served good breakfasts and lousy dinners and fed hundreds of people every day. The waitress who brought my coffee looked so glazed that she wouldn't recognize her own mother. I felt the knots in my stomach begin to loosen while I sipped and stirred. Fifteen minutes later I heard the sirens wailing on Probasco Street.

Chapter 4

I looped through the concrete spiral of the Riverview Hospital parking garage for five minutes before I found a space. I turned off the key and stared out the window at the rear of the hospital. In a yawning hole in the ground, men were setting up forms, wiring steel reinforcing rods together, and pouring concrete. Eventually there would be another wing on a building that already looked like a collision between the Ambassador Hotel and the Dallas Airport. I wondered if the Administrative suite was going to find its way into the new wing. I tried not to think about Barry and his briefcase.

I took the yellow sheet out of my pocket and held it up beside the half-page of the xeroxed letter from my wallet. *Do you make her lick your balls Doctor? The quick brown fox jumps over the lazy dog.* Jesus Christ. I looked at the construction crew a while longer, and then I went back to the letters and the nuances of the type-styles. They weren't even close. They were both done in elite type, but so were half a million church bulletins.

I locked the two sheets in the glove compartment and walked through the parking garage to the hospital. I went down a flight of stairs and followed a series of plastic signs that said *Cafeteria*. I could smell the place before I got there. Inside the dining-room door a black woman was picking the soiled napkins and empty sugar-packets off the dirty food trays. She put the trays full of washable stuff on a conveyor belt that ran into a hole in the wall. We exchanged blank stares, and I walked over to the serving line. The meat loaf looked like you could caulk a boat with it. I got coffee and a ham sandwich and sat down where I could watch the employees passing the cash register.

In the next quarter-hour at least fifty employees came through the cafeteria line, sliding their trays as humorlessly as acolytes in a processional. With a few exceptions, the people who sat together wore the same kinds of uniforms. Several tables were full of nurses. The people from Surgery with their hairnets and green uniforms sat clustered together in a corner. The Housekeeping staff, mostly black, sat glumly at the far end of the room. There weren't any doctors; they ate someplace else. You couldn't find a more rigid caste system this side of Calcutta.

Joyce Gruber came through the line by herself. She was wearing a nurse's uniform with white hospital stockings and no makeup. She looked like she'd been up all night. She was in her thirties and beginning to put on some womanly weight that looked good on her. She by-passed a table of nurses and sat, essentially alone, at another table with two fiftyish women who looked like they worked in the Business Office. After nodding hello, they ignored her.

During the next fifteen minutes a few nurses said, "Hello, Joyce," as they passed her with their trays on their way to the conveyor belt. None of them stopped to talk. Several men ogled her from a distance, but nobody ambled over to share a cup of coffee. It was hard to pin down exactly what she radiated, but you knew in your loins that if you made love with her she'd have you arching your back and baying at the moon. She also looked lonely as a leper.

When the two business-office women picked up their trays and headed for the door, I carried my coffee cup over and sat down across from her. I could feel the glances coming our way from the others in the cafeteria. "Miss Gruber?"

She waited several seconds before she said, "Yes?" She looked at me the way you look at the mailman who brings you a registered letter. Maybe it's the Irish Sweepstakes. Maybe it's your results back from the lab.

I said, "Barry Alspach killed himself last night."

She frowned. "Who are you?"

"My name is Chandler. I'm a private investigator."

"You're kidding."

I shook my head and kept looking at her. Her eyes were the giveaway. Someone had told her a long time ago that a man was going to come along and carry her off and take care of everything. She still believed it, but she was getting a little desperate about it. After a second or two, she remembered what I'd told her. She said, "Who's Barry Alspach?"

"He's the Administrative Intern." She shook her head. It didn't mean a thing to her. I said, "He was a tall awkward-looking kid who worked in Administration. He had sandy hair."

"Oh, him. I know who you mean. He killed himself?"

"Yes. He slit his wrists."

She winced like someone who's seen a news story about famine victims. "Why are you telling me this?"

"Because he did it for a reason. I'm trying to find out what that reason is."

"Well... Okay, I hear what you're saying. But I don't know him." I didn't say anything. She said, "Look, the only time I ever talked to him was when he came up to the unit to look at the kardex..."

"What's a kardex?"

"Just a minute. You don't think that *I* had anything to do with this, do you?"

I said, "I think that Barry was a naive kid. I think he found out something that he couldn't handle." Her eyes were beginning to glaze over with polite boredom. I felt like an idiot, but I kept going. "It may have been about somebody that he worshipped from afar. He found out that they were doing something ugly and criminal, and he didn't know what to do with the knowledge, and he killed himself."

Joyce was looking down at her plate. I fought off a wild urge to try to shore up the nonsense I'd just constructed. If she had half the sense that I knew she had, she'd give me about thirty seconds to get out of there before she called Security. But she didn't. When she looked up at me, her eyes were cold and frightened, and her teeth were clenched with loathing. She said, "I don't know what you're getting at. I don't know this Barry, and I don't know you."

She stood up and started to pick up her tray. I said, "Can you type?"

She looked at me like I'd stripped naked and stood on my head. "Can I *type*? My God, what are you... you're crazy. You're just crazy." She handed her tray blindly to the black woman and walked out the door.

I got another cup of coffee and paid another twenty cents for it. The chair where Joyce had been sitting was askew, and I shoved it back under the table where it belonged. I sat down, realized that I'd forgotten to pick up cream or sugar, and trekked back through the cafeteria line to get some. I felt like I'd just shaken down a fourth-grade girl for her lunch money.

I was tearing the sugar-packet into tiny strips

and waiting for my insides to relax when Oberding sat down across from me. He looked at the confetti I was making. "You nervous, Chandler?"

"I'm never nervous when the police are on the scene, Lieutenant."

He pulled out a pack of Luckies that looked like it'd been used as a doorstop. "Still the old smart mouth, eh?"

"Somebody has to do it. You here to see your proctologist?"

He lit a cigarette and exhaled through his nostrils. It had been years since I'd seen anybody do that. He was moon-faced, and he'd been a fat kid when he was younger. I wondered how old he was. It was hard to tell with cops. He said, "If I find any of your prints over on Probasco Street, I'll haul your ass in as an accessory to murder."

"You dusting your girlfriend's apartment? It's probably a good idea, because..."

"Shut your mouth, piss-ant. We get a tip from some fucker won't give his name. We find a dead kid in an apartment where the neighbor says she seen a tall skinny guy going in and out this morning. The kid's parents up in New York say that he works here, and you turn up in the cafeteria. I ought to run your ass in."

"Oh, come on, Lieutenant. All of us tall guys look alike."

He started to yell at me, but he remembered where he was. Everybody within thirty feet was dawdling over coffee cups and sneaking furtive glances in our direction. Oberding said, "You smart-mouth me one more time and I'll take you downtown on general principles. Now what the fuck are you doing here?"

"If I were dumb enough to answer that kind of question, I wouldn't be able to make a nickel. You know what I do, and you know that people hire me because they don't want their business spread all over town." Oberding was still breathing hard, but he was cooling off a little. I said, "I'll be as cooperative as I can if I don't get treated like a bum in the drunk tank. If you tell me what's going on, maybe I can help."

He blew more smoke out of his nose, and wispy curls hung around his nostrils. "Bastards like you piss me off. Somebody plunks down a few bucks and you think you've got the right to fuck around with everybody."

"Then that makes two of us, Lieutenant."

Oberding stubbed out his cigarette and reached for another. He looked exhausted and angry. He said, "You know this kid Barry Alspach?"

"Who's he?"

"He's the kid I was telling you about that works here. Anyway, he shot himself last night."

"I thought you said it was murder."

"That's what I'm checking out." We stared at each other for a few seconds. Finally he said, "Ah, piss on it. He probably did it himself. He didn't shoot himself, neither."

I sipped on my coffee and Oberding sucked on his cigarette. I began to listen to the hum of cafeteria conversation that had been droning in the background. After a while Oberding perked up out of his reverie. "But somebody called. Wouldn't nobody call unless there was something wrong."

"Maybe people just don't want to get involved any more."

"Yeah. And maybe somebody's suppressing evidence for his fucking precious client."

I said, "I don't frame anybody. And I don't bury any smoking guns. If I find anything that connects with this, I'll let you know."

"You better." Oberding stood up and drew himself up to full height. He was about five-five. He walked off without saying goodbye.

I finished my coffee, left the cafeteria, and walked upstairs to the lobby. The visitors in the vinyl chairs were mostly women. A gaggle of teenage girls in pink uniforms were all talking to each other at once while they peeled off winter coats and gloves. Their badges said *Riverview Hospital School of Nursing*. I didn't see any up-and-coming Joyce Grubers in the group. They looked like their idea of excitement would be to sneak a six-pack of beer into the dormitory.

I went into the gift shop and bought two packs of peanuts. I was going to be hungry as a tundra wolf in a couple of hours. The place was full of get-well cards, baseball mugs and pennants, and all kinds of bedside doodads with round yellow smile-faces on them. A man wearing a clerical collar and a badge that said *Chaplain Trainee* was browsing through a rack of paperbacks. The books had collages of happy faces and sunrises on the covers, with titles like *God's Plan for America*. It was the kind of place that made me want to light a cigar and drink bourbon out of a paper sack.

I crossed the lobby and walked into the Administrative suite. I was beginning to feel like an old hand around the place. Joan looked up with anxious eyes when I walked in, but Siehl hollered at me before she could say anything. "Hey, I was wondering when you were going to come back. C'mon in." He looked rattled. "Sit down, glad you're here. You heard about Barry?"

"I heard he was dead. What happened?"

"He killed himself. Jesus, can you imagine?" He lit a cigarette. He kept clenching and unclenching his free hand.

"Why did he do it?"

Siehl feigned bug-eyed exasperation. "That's a wierd-ass peculiar god-damn question coming from you." I didn't say anything. He said, "I thought you were really smart."

"No, I'm just persistent. Why did he do it?"

"Because he was writing the *letters*! Jesus Christ!"

"Really?"

Siehl rolled his eyes heavenward and made imploring gestures like Tevye in *Fiddler on the Roof*. He said, "Boy, it's a goddamned good thing you didn't have to figure anything out. Look – I hired you. Barry met you. He knew we were serious, and he got scared, and he went home and killed himself."

I said, "What about Joyce?"

"Joyce? Oh, shit." Siehl winced and looked down at the rug. "She's just a flaky broad."

"You're sure of that?"

He leaned toward me and lowered his voice. "See, I had a little fling with Joyce last summer. Believe me, she's flaky,"

I said, "I hope nobody in this hospital has the clap."

Siehl glared at me. "Okay. Enough of this shit. This thing is over, and I want four hundred dollars back."

"It isn't over." We stared at each other like a couple of gangsters in a movie. I said, "Barry didn't write those letters. Parker's troubles are going to get worse instead of better."

"What makes you so sure?"

I thought about telling Siehl about the typefaces, but I didn't think that he could keep his mouth shut. I said, "It doesn't make sense. Why would Barry write moonstruck letters to needle a doctor about his sex life?" As I was saying it, a thought slid in like a cold block of granite. I wondered if Barry's father was a doctor.

Siehl said, "Of course it doesn't make any sense. What the hell does?"

"Your friend Joyce Gruber has something on her mind. I made her cry with a couple of flimsy innuendoes. She looks like she's had enough bad experiences with men to make her sour on the subject. I think Joyce, or some other woman in the same boat, is much more likely to write smutty letters to Richard Parker than Barry was."

Siehl shaped the ash on his cigarette by rolling it between his fingers in the ashtray. "Are you holding out on me?"

"I'm telling you as much as I can."

"As you *can*? Who the hell do you think you're working for?"

"You hired me to do a job, not to free-associate. I don't think that the job's done."

Siehl stubbed out his cigarette firmly. "Well, it is. Right now. I want you to leave, and I want four hundred dollars back."

"This is Tuesday. I'll send it to you on Friday."

"What kind of shit-ass arrangement is that?"

"I'm betting that by Friday you're going to want me back worse than ever." I got up and walked out, trying not to grin. I sounded like somebody's jilted sweetheart on *The Edge of Night*. I stopped in front of Joan's desk. "Will you meet me for a drink after work?" She looked flustered and darted a glance at the door to Siehl's office. My adrenalin was cranked up too high, and my stomach began to clench with an acidic craving. I said, "Call me if you can," and stormed out into the hall.

I tore open one of the packs of peanuts and wolfed them down. My stomach relaxed, and I started to think again. I wondered for the hundredth time how people could stand to eat the crap that was served in restaurants and cafeterias. I decided that I'd make myself a good dinner in the evening. It looked like I wasn't going to have a lot of other things to do.

It was only two o'clock. I could drive to Chicago, shoot a roll of pictures, or sit in a bar and write limericks. I could work out at the dojo or swim in an indoor pool. But I kept thinking about Barry and his briefcase and the beer bottles. I felt guilty as hell. And beyond that the whole business felt like a bad case of *coitus interruptus*. I munched on the other pack of peanuts and decided that Siehl's hundred dollars entitled me to poke around until five o'clock. Maybe I could find an embittered woman hunched over a typewriter muttering obscenities about Richard Parker under her breath.

I walked down the hall and into the office labeled *Assistant Administrator*. There was no secretary at the desk in the outer office, and the phone was buzzing and blinking with an incoming call. I heard Gibbs at his desk, talking on the other line and ignoring the repetitive buzzing. He was saying, "I wouldn't worry about it, Mr. Ross. I don't think they'll even ask us. If they do, I'll just talk to the editor and take care of it." The buzzing stopped, and I could hear him more clearly. "Yes, I'm sure of it. I'll take care of it. Yes, sir." He sounded as fervent as a revivalist on the phone with Billy Graham. When he hung up, I stepped into his office. "Mr. Gibbs?"

He scanned me briefly and then pretended to read a sheet of paper. "Who are you and what do you want?"

"My name is Chandler. I knew Barry Alspach."

"And what were you doing in Mr. Siehl's office this morning?"

"The same thing I'm doing now."

He still didn't look up. "And how did you know Barry?"

"I met him once. I liked him. He wasn't afraid of eye contact."

Gibbs slowly assumed a theatrical look of bemusement. "Eye contact is a form of non-verbal communication which is used to indicate interest. Or lack of it." Now he was staring at me. His skin had a dead-fish pallor that made his eyes look watery.

I said, "You were Barry's Preceptor, weren't you?"

"You obviously know that I was."

"What was he working on?"

Gibbs stroked his cheek with a forefinger. "How can that possibly interest you?"

"If you don't tell me, it'll sure as hell interest Art Brookshire at the *Post*." Gibbs didn't jump, but his eyes looked like they'd frozen over. I said, "Barry was a nice kid who was trying to launch a decent career. His whole life revolved around his internship and this hospital. Last night he killed himself. Something happened here to cause that." Gibbs didn't move a muscle. I said, "Now, you and I can talk about Barry, or you and I and Art Brookshire can have a nice friendly chat. Which would you like?"

Gibbs looked at me steadily, probing for a twitch or a falter. I did my best to forget that I'd met

Art Brookshire once at a poker game. Gibbs finally sighed and said, "All right. You asked me what Barry was looking into?" I nodded. He said, "I assigned him to do a study of disposable equipment versus the cost of sterilizing and autoclaving." This time I stared and looked for a twitch. At least Gibbs had lost some of his snotty attitude. He said, "If you want proof, I can show you the memo I wrote when I made the assignment. I also have a copy of Barry's preliminary report."

I took in a deep breath and let it out slowly. *Disposable equipment versus the cost of autoclaving.* Chandler and his instinct for vital issues. I said, "Do you have any idea why Barry killed himself?"

Gibbs smirked. "I rather imagine that it had something to do with his relationship with his father." He leaned back and assumed a face like a Japanese Commandant interrogating a prisoner. I wondered if he had a normal expression. He said, "What's your real interest in all of this?"

"Jesus H. Christ, are you still around?" Gibbs and I looked up at Siehl, who was standing in the doorway with some papers in his hand. He said, "You're supposed to be gone. Get the hell out of here."

Gibbs said, "Is this man working for you?" He looked alarmed. Maybe that was his natural state.

Siehl said, "Hell, yes. He's a detective. I hired him to... for some private business."

Gibbs stood up. His voice was icy. "I am going to call our Security Chief. I suggest that you had better be out of here...

I said, "Shucks, We were just getting acquainted." I stepped past Siehl and headed out into the hall.

I drove downtown and parked in my rented spot in the garage under the Kroger Building. I walked across the street and had a bowl of soup at the hippie restaurant. It was one of the few places in town where every dish wasn't boiled into tastelessness or fried in a tub of grease. The people who ran the restaurant lived together in a commune. I wondered how long they could stay in business before the inevitable egotism and overlording would take its toll.

I walked up the block to the Railway Clerks' Building. There hadn't been a railway clerk near the place for twenty years. Most of the offices were rented to the AFL-CIO Labor Council and to individual unions for headquarters. My office was on the third floor, down the hall from the sheet-metal workers and the Human Relations Commission. I'd promised myself that some day I'd go into the Human Relations office and find out what the hell they did.

My waiting room was empty as a nursing-home parking lot on Visitor's Day. The pencil that I'd put under one of the chairs to check up on the cleaning guy was still there. Maybe he'd dusted it. In the magazine rack there were two old copies of Newsweek and the January 1976 issue of Esquire with the Dubious Achievement Awards. I reminded myself that the 1977 issue was going to be available before long.

I unlocked the inner door and stepped into the office. The place was full of pent-up steam heat. Like Barry's office. I opened the window a crack. The brick wall on the other side of the airshaft was covered with a lumpy layer of soot that looked like it would have grown into Spanish moss in a warmer climate.

There was some mail on the floor that had been stuffed in through a slot in the door. I picked it up and sat down at the desk. I threw away the offers to subscribe to *Business Week* and the Time-Life Book Club. The others were pleas to join Common Cause and to contribute to the United Negro College Fund. I threw them away, too. To hell with everybody. I sat and stared at the empty bookshelf sitting by the wall. I had thought about putting together a reference library of phone books, city directories, almanacs, business and professional directories, and maybe a dictionary. Someday I'd have to do that. But it didn't matter.

And it didn't matter that a nice clumsy kid named Barry Alspach had slit his wrists and then tried to save himself a little too late to keep from bleeding to death. It didn't matter that a lonely nurse was getting so bitter and crazy that she was probably writing hate letters to the doctor who'd left her hanging. It didn't matter that a bunch of high-priced executives were screwing around and trying to outmaneuver each other to see who was going to be the Big Kahuna at Riverview Hospital and everyplace else.

And it didn't matter that a cranky individual

named Chandler was sitting at a government-surplus desk watching the afternoon gloom gather in a dingy building and feeling pissed-off at the world. He'd earned his hundred bucks and he could sleep the sleep of the just.

The phone rang, and I grabbed it like a life-preserver. "Hello?"

"Hello. This is Joan."

"Lady, I am glad you called. Where are you?"

"I'm still at work." I looked at my watch. It was four o'clock. She said, "Mr. Siehl is out of the office. I called your home number, but I got that recorded-message machine. Your voice sounds awful on that tape. Are you busy?"

"I'm sitting here watching my fingernails grow. How about that drink?"

"Oh, I can't... Listen, Frank – may I call you Frank?"

"Don't ask dumb questions. Of course you can."

"Where did you go this morning?"

I looked out the window at a pigeon fluttering around in the air-shaft. "It's better if you don't know."

"I wish you wouldn't try to be so cagey all the time." She began to sound exasperated. "You asked me where Barry lived, and you ran out the door. Then the police came to Mr. Ross's office about an hour later to say that he'd committed suicide. Then when you came back, you were sure that Barry hadn't written the letters, but you wouldn't tell Mr. Siehl why. You must have found something over there."

"Have you told Siehl any of this?"

"No, I – I guess I assume that you know what you're doing."

"If I send you a dollar a day, will you call me once in a while and say that again?"

"You sound awfully depressed."

"*Frustrated* is more like it. My blood sugar gets all screwed up. How well did you know Barry Alspach?"

"I guess I thought you knew. Barry and I were buddies. We started working here on the same day." She paused for a few seconds. "You know, I can't really believe that he's dead. I keep expecting him to walk in here." I waited for her to go on. There's no reply to those sad words. She said, "And I know that he didn't write those letters."

"He didn't. Did he ever say anything about his father?"

"Let me think... I know that he didn't get along with his father very well. I think that he was trying to prove something to his father by getting into hospital administration."

"Was his father an administrator?"

"No. I think Barry said he was a District Sales Manager for Eastman Kodak."

I said, "Oh, for God's sake."

Joan sounded alarmed. "Does that mean something?"

"Not exactly, but it fits a pattern. I've known two other Kodak salesmen. One of them shot his wife, and the other one shot himself."

We listened to the hum in the phone wires. She

said, "You sound bitter. Why?"

"I just hate to see people get screwed over. Salesmen are a bunch of average guys who've been fed a lot of crap about being aggressive. So they're hard on their families. And on each other and on themselves. It's the same at Xerox and IBM."

"And Procter & Gamble."

"Why do you say that?"

"My husband works there."

I could hear a siren yelping in the street outside. It was getting damn dark in the office, but I felt too lazy to get up and switch on a light. I toyed with a kink in the phone cord. Joan said, "What are you going to do?"

"I don't know. I don't give a tiny god-damn about Parker and his hate mail. But I made Barry a partner in the investigation, and now he's dead, and I'm closed out of it."

"You did what with Barry?"

"I bet him that he could figure out who wrote the letters. God *damn* it. 'When a man's partner is killed...'"

"'...you're supposed to do something about it." She sighed, "Frank, listen. I think you'd better be careful to sort out what's really *you* from what's left over from a lot of old movies. You could drive yourself crazy."

"Okay. Thanks, really. I'll try to keep that in mind." We let a few seconds roll by. I said, "Joan?"

"Yes?"

"Meet me for a drink tomorrow?"

"Mmmm. I'm going to get in trouble if I keep talking to you. I'll think about it. Bye-bye."

I sat there for a while with the receiver in my left hand, holding the phone button down with a forefinger. I wanted to call her back. I wanted to take her someplace where we could eat crab legs and smooch in a secluded booth and blow Siehl's hundred dollars on wine. Instead I was going to stop at a grocery store and pick up some sausages and a six-pack of beer. *Procter & Gamble.* I wondered why she was working.

"Waitin' for a call, Chief?"

A tall, broad-shouldered man was standing in the doorway. He was my height, younger, and he had a few pounds on me, He was hawk-faced, from what I could see. It was dark and shadowy, and I didn't like being caught with my shirttails out. I stood up, cradled the phone, and switched on the light.

"Or are you just sittin' here jerkin' off in the moonlight?"

He *was* a big son of a bitch. He was wearing a leather car coat and a shirt that was open far enough to let a square foot of his chest hang out. He had a cannibalistic-looking silver-and-bone choker around his neck. I said, "You're cute as a bug."

"Ain't I pretty?" He strolled over to the window and looked out at the bricks. "Nice view."

We listened to each other breathing. I said, "The barber college is up the street. Or were you looking for the vasectomy clinic?"

"You ain't very friendly, Chief." He rested a

haunch on my desk. He looked up at me suddenly, as though a thought had just struck him. He was grinning a cocky grin, and the whites showed all around his eyes. "Hey! How'd you like to see some Tae Kwon Do?"

"I never thought much of that Korean stuff. All feet. Two guys come at you, and you'll split yourself up to the gizzard."

"It gets the job done." He craned around to look at the doodles on my desk blotter. I yawned. He jiggled around in a jerky rhythm, mostly with shoulders and knees, while he sat there. His hands were big as ping-pong paddles. Out in the hall a door clicked shut as somebody locked up for the night. He kept studying the doodles like the Dead Sea Scrolls. Finally he said, "What was you lookin' for up at that hospital today?"

"Who's asking?"

"Jus' me, Chief." He put his left hand on his hip and scrunched his coat back so I could see the .357 magnum hanging in a shoulder-holster.

I said, "Stick that up your ass and you'll give yourself a real enema."

At least that got him to look up at me. "I don' believe you said that."

"Be careful when you shoot that thing. The recoil can make it jump back and pop you in the forehead. I knew a guy in the Army..."

"Don't tell me about guns, fucker."

"Of course, with a revolver you get a lot of gas leakage...

"Shut up!" He stood up and let his hands hang at his sides, like Clint Eastwood.

I said, "Touchy, touchy. Get the hell out of here so I can lock up."

He muttered *cocksucker* and stomped over to my empty bookcase. It was made of three-quarter-inch pine. He made a fist and smashed down on the top shelf. It broke with a crack. He breathed out loudly through his nose. "Smart-mouth cocksucker. Stay the fuck away from that hospital!"

He clomped out and slammed the hall door. I listened to him storm down the stairs, resisting an urge to race him to the first floor in the elevator. Whatever else he might be, he didn't exactly look like a pushover.

I dragged the broken bookcase out into the hall, where I'd found it a year earlier along with a wastebasket and other remnants of somebody's failed enterprise. Then I headed for home. There wasn't anything else to do.

Chapter 5

The next morning I ran two miles before breakfast. The cold air made my lungs ache. I thought about letting my beard grow for the winter, but I decided to wait until I could get out of town for a while. I looked seedy enough without a week's stubble. There were no lovers out necking in their cars. A pretty girl wearing a puffy red goose-down jacket was walking a great dane in the park. I felt randy as a goat.

  I sprinted the last two blocks home. I showered, dressed, and got the breakfast stuff out of the refrigerator. Nobody had called the night before to beg me to come back to Riverview. Joan hadn't sneaked over for a midnight tryst. I had finished the Doctorow novel, and I wanted a copy of *Scoundrel Time*. While the bacon fried, I added *Hellman* to the list that I kept on top of the refrigerator. The other entries were *Hustling* and *Sjowall and Wahloo*. I scrambled the eggs and ate everything ravenously.

I was having a second cup of coffee when the phone rang. It was Richard Parker.

"Chandler?"

"'Morning, Doctor."

"I understand that Siehl has discharged you. I want you to work for me."

"What happened?"

Parker snorted over the phone and then lowered his voice. "Whoever is doing this thing is getting out of hand. There were calls coming to my house until three o'clock this morning. My wife is nearly hysterical. You've got to stop them."

I tried to keep the grin out of my voice. "I'll be glad to. In all fairness, though, you may not need me. The phone company can trace a creep call if you let them know what's going on."

"I've tried that, Chandler. They traced the calls last night. They were coming from the hospital. There's a centrex system, and they couldn't trace beyond that."

"Why didn't you leave your phone off the hook?"

"Damn it, Chandler. I'm not going to beg. If you don't want the job..."

I said, "I'll look for your caller. I have a fair idea of who it might be. Have there been any more letters?"

"No. I want you to make this fast, Chandler." I told him my rates and asked for a retainer. He groused about it but said he'd put a check in the mail. I told him that I'd call him as soon as I had anything solid, and we hung up. My juices were flowing like crazy. I felt as high as a teeny-bopper with two dexamils and a coca-cola under his belt. I started to throw on my coat and head out the door, but I decided to call Joan first.

I called the main switchboard at the hospital instead of Siehl's private number. They connected me, and she answered the phone with that gorgeous voice of hers. "Mr. Siehl's office."

"'Morning, Beautiful. Can you talk?"

"Oh, yes, but nobody ever listens... Hello, Frank."

"Is Siehl there?"

"No, he's in a meeting, and I'm just typing. I'm glad you called. I'm getting buggy."

"How would you like to help in a red-hot investigation?"

"Really? Did you decide to go ahead on your own?"

"I was spared the agony of deciding. Now I need some scuttlebutt on Joyce Gruber. Nothing formal. You have the inside track with the people down in Personnel. Can you snoop around and see if she's been involved in any screwy behavior?"

"Do you mean her personal behavior, or on the job, or..."

"Anything. Can you find out right away and call me back?"

"Do I get another offer for a cup of coffee out of this? Or do you just go around promiscuously offering..."

"Scotch. Lunch at La Normandie."

She was quiet for a long time. Finally she said, "You know, I think you're halfway serious."

"Not halfway."

She put a suburban-sensible tone back into her voice and said, "Well, thank you. I can't go to lunch, but I will go to Personnel. Are you at home or at the office?"

"At home. People keep busting up my furniture when I'm at the office."

"What?"

"Never mind. Just find out what you can and call me back right away."

We said good-bye and hung up. I made another cup of coffee and got some English muffins out of the freezer. I made a real production out of toasting and eating them. I dawdled over them for as long as possible, and then I rinsed off a week's worth of accumulated dishes and stuck them in the dishwasher. Time seemed to have gotten its foot caught under a glacier. I paced and fumed and finally took down a copy of *The Best and the Brightest* that I'd been reading in fits and starts for three years. I'd lost all track of where I'd stopped, so I flipped back through the pages. *MacNamara. Dean Rusk. John Paton Davies.* I forced myself to concentrate, and I finally got absorbed in the machinations around the Tonkin Gulf incident when the phone rang.

Joan sounded wound-up with an excitement of her own. "I think I might have something! I talked to Louise – do you remember she's the one who files all the Personnel records?"

"What did she say?"

"Well, there was a real mess here last September. It must have happened just before I got here. There was an Orderly named Oliver Jackson, and he'd worked on Joyce's unit for years. You know? Anyway, she fired him."

"What for?"

"Well, the technical reason was because he came in late one day. But when they looked in his file there were six months' worth of warnings and reprimands from Joyce to him. I mean exactly six months. It was as though she set out a campaign to get rid of him."

"Did he try to fight it?"

"Apparently he talked to the Personnel Director about it, but it didn't help. She'd followed all of the procedures to the letter, and they couldn't do anything. Louise says that he was a real nice guy. And she said that they can do that to just about anybody if they really want to."

"Swell. Was there anything else?"

"The only other thing that Louise could think of was that there was an LPN who complained about Joyce shifting her schedule around last month. I mean that's all she could remember as far as business was concerned. She went on for a long time about all the men that Joyce has slept with. She mentioned Doctor Parker. "

"Did she mention Siehl?"

"No! Did they really?"

"Your friend Louise probably figures that you're sleeping with him, and she didn't want to make you jealous."

"Oh, you've got to be kidding... Does she really think that?"

"It seems to be the national pastime. And your Louise is a doll. Can you find out..."

"I'll bet you want to know where Oliver Jackson lives."

"I ought to do your typing and give you my license. Where does he live?"

"It's 2240-B Winneste. Do you know where that is?"

"I sure do, and I pity the poor bastard already. Thanks a million for this. When can we have that drink?"

She didn't answer right away. Finally she said, "It's sounding better all the time."

We said good-bye again and hung up. I grabbed my coat and bounded out to the car like a kid who just got ten dollars for his birthday.

Winneste Avenue curved up a long hill from the industrial flats that surrounded the Procter & Gamble plant. In the late '50's the city had used a huge chunk of urban-renewal money to tear down the black ghetto that sat next to the downtown district and built replacement ghettos out in the boondocks. Winton Hills was one of them. It looked like a street of model public housing tenements: pseudo-colonial, pseudo-tudor, pseudo-cottage, and blockhouse. There were broken-down chain-link fences between the rows of townhouses that had been intended to keep the kids off the grass. That hadn't lasted long. The brick facing was starting to fall off some of the older buildings, exposing patches of tarpaper and fiberboard.

I parked in front of 2240-B and got out of the car. Two tiny black kids in ratty-looking leisure-suit jackets gaped at me from the yard. Six teenage boys cruised by in a banged-up Oldsmobile with a Playboy rabbit sticker on the back bumper. A very old woman was pulling a two-wheeled metal grocery tote-basket up the sidewalk across the street. I had thought about calling before I came over, but had decided against it. On the phone I'd be just another honky bill-collector.

I walked to the door and pushed the doorbell. Nothing much seemed to happen. I banged on the door. The two tiny kids wobbled over to the foot of the stoop and kept staring at me. I said, "Hi," but they didn't change expressions.

A woman opened the door while I was looking at the kids. She said, "May I he'p you?" with exaggerated courtesy. She was about forty with prominent cheekbones and impish, ornery eyes. She also looked like she wouldn't take any crap from anybody.

I said, "Is Mr. Jackson home?"

"Who?"

I had forgotten my ghetto etiquette. I said, "My name is Frank Chandler, and I'm an investigator. I'm working on a case that involves the people who fired your husband from Riverview Hospital."

"What make you think he's my husband?" She had a terrific grin.

I stuck my hands in my pockets and looked down at the ground. I felt like a rookie Fuller Brush salesman. I said, "I think I'll go home and go back to bed and start over. Are you Mrs. Jackson?"

"You won't accomplish nothing if you sleep all day, son."

"Ma'am, I probably won't accomplish anything if I run around like a chicken with its head cut off. I just keep poking along regardless. I am investigating a situation at Riverview Hospital, and I think that Mr. Jackson knows some things that can help me."

"I believed you the first time, son. I just wondered how your manners was. Are you from the Dee-Oh-Ell?"

It took me a few seconds to fish that one out. *Department of Labor.* I said, "No. I have a private license."

"Then what good can it do my husband to talk to you? You can't get him no job back."

She wasn't kidding about that. I said, "You're probably right. Your husband got a raw deal, and he's probably stuck with it. But if I'm successful, the people who fired him won't have another chance to hurt anybody else."

"It wasn't no people. It was just that nurse."

My feet were starting to get cold on the concrete stoop. I said, "May I talk to your husband,

Ma'am?"

"He's not here. He's working."

"Where?"

She shook her head, and I saw some bitterness in her eyes. "It ain't no hospital. Ollie worked in a hospital for fifteen years, but he couldn't get no hospital job after he been fired. He's up at the Sak-Pak."

"Beg pardon?"

"It's up in Norwood. They makes paper bags."

"Thank you. If I find out anything about what happened to your husband's job, I'll try to set the record straight."

She looked down the street at the ugly brick facades. "I've heard a lot of promises in my life, son. Don't make no promises you can't keep."

The two little kids were tussling over a pop bottle in the front yard. I said, "Are they yours?"

"No, our kids is grown. They're from next door. I teach them at the Head Start."

"Lucky kids. Good-bye, Mrs. Jackson." I walked back to the car, turned around in the nearest driveway, and drove back down Winneste toward the factories. She watched from her doorway for as long as I could see her in the rear-view mirror.

I drove to a restaurant in Norwood, slugged down a cup of coffee, and looked up *Sak-Pak, Inc* in the phone book. It was an unfamiliar street, and when I got back to the car I had to dig a city map out of the glove compartment. It was buried under a ragged handful of crackly receipts from credit-card gas purchases, scribbled notes, and several traffic tickets for failing to get my safety-inspection sticker renewed. I located the Sak-Pak street and nosed the Fairlane out of the parking lot.

The factory was in a godforsaken region behind the big General Motors stamping plant. The paved street ended, and I drove warily up a heavily-rutted access road that wandered among several little sweatshops. There were six concrete-block buildings where people assembled valves, universal joints, and plastic components for god-knows-what. Sak-Pak was tucked in among them, with only a small dirty sign to identify itself. I parked in a muddy lot alongside eight other cars that looked even older and more beat-up than mine. It was ten minutes before noon.

The building was half cinderblock and half quonset hut. I opened a door in the cinderblock part, and a wave of heat whooshed out. The place was full of pallets loaded with four-foot stacks of folded brown paper. They were arranged in rows on the floor and stacked on massive shelves on the walls up to a thirty-foot ceiling. There were no windows. The building was lit with weak fluorescent lights, and it was dreary as a prison.

I followed a tow-motor path that was marked on the floor with chewed-up strips of reflective tape. A loud pounding noise came from the quonset-hut end of the building. I passed a time-clock and a row of benches. A hand-lettered sign said *Onley use the phone on breaks and lunch. No long distance.* I stifled an urge to call Seattle and stepped into the quonset hut.

There was an assembly line organized in a long U-shape. Down one side of the building four eight-foot-wide rolls of brown paper were fed through a toonerville-trolley apparatus with lots of exposed gears and drive-chains. A pump sucked glue out of a fifty-gallon drum and squeezed it onto the edges of the paper. A paper cutter that looked like a hydraulic guillotine slammed down every five seconds and chopped off a six-foot-wide brown sack. Four white men who were filthy with ink and grease tended the machine.

The sacks slid across the building on a conveyor-belt and were fed into a forty-foot-long drying oven. Heat rolled off the oven in waves. Two women standing at the other end of the oven reached into a slot and yanked out the sacks that had been dried. They looked them over quickly, stacked them in piles of five, and shoved them with effort across a wide table. A tall black man folded the piles awkwardly and stacked them on a pallet. He had to be Oliver Jackson. He was the only black person in the place.

The rhythm of the activity was interrupted when one of the women yelled, "*Re*-pair!" and heaved one of the bags to the side. Jackson hurried around the table to chuck it onto a different pallet in the corner. For the next few minutes the intact bags alternated with *re*-pairs, and Jackson began to sweat and breathe heavily as he ran back and forth. He looked like he wasn't in good shape.

An ugly squawk sounded through the plant, and the assembly line shut down for lunch. Jackson and the two women kept sorting and stacking while the backlog of sacks rolled out of the oven. The women helped Jackson fold and stack the last few sacks. One of the women had high cheekbones and a good figure, and she could have been damned attractive. Instead she looked exhausted. Jackson wiped his forehead and said, "Hot doggies," and both of the women smiled. The attractive one didn't have any teeth.

The three of them walked past me in the doorway without looking up. I said, "Mr. Jackson?"

He jerked around, startled. "Who are you?"

"My name is Chandler, and I'm a private investigator. I'd like to talk with you. Can I buy you lunch?"

He rubbed his knuckles across his chin with a scratchy sound. "I ain't got time." He started toward the bench where the others were eating sandwiches out of lunchboxes and paper bags.

I said, "I'm investigating Joyce Gruber." He stopped and looked back at me suspiciously. I said, "Let's get out of this dungeon and get something to eat."

He said, "I can't go out to no lunch, and that's a fact. We ain't got but half an hour."

"Is there someplace here where we can talk?"

"I won't make no promises about talkin', neither. But I'll hear what you got to say." He walked over to the bench, picked up a small paper bag, and motioned me to follow him back into the assembly-line room.

The other employees sneaked glances at us. Jackson walked to a corner where pallets were stacked up. He had a slight limp. He picked up a six-foot-square sheet of torn brown paper off the floor and laid it over the stack of pallets so that we'd have a halfway-clean place to sit.

I said, "What the hell do they make here?"

"Shippin' bags for mattresses. We're runnin' king-size today. They're mean."

I looked at the now-quiet assembly line. There were scraps of paper and gobs of glue everywhere. There were windows in the quonset-hut walls, but they were covered with metal security screens. I said, "Ever had a fire?"

"Lord, I hope not."

He dug a sandwich out of his lunch-bag and chewed on it unenthusiastically. A minute or two went by. I finally said, "Mr. Jackson, I don't have much to horse-trade with. I'm investigating a situation at Riverview Hospital that I think involves Joyce Gruber. I've heard that she fired you for no good reason." Jackson didn't say anything. I said, "I need to know if it fits into a pattern. I can't promise you a thing, but if she's who I'm looking for, I'll do what I can to get you your job back. Why did she fire you?"

He smiled to himself. "'Cause I come in late."

"I heard she'd been setting you up for six months."

Jackson chewed wordlessly on his sandwich until he finished it. He pulled an apple out of his sack. I felt a twinge of hunger and realized that it had been a long time since breakfast. We sat and listened to the hiss of the gas-jets in the oven. Finally he said, "I hate this fuckin' place."

"You'd be crazy if you didn't. Why did she fire you?"

"Because I seen her. At that party."

"What party?"

He spoke slowly, groping for where to begin. "She give this party, see? She invite' everybody on the unit, but it wasn't like no hospital party. I mean we was all invited, but it wasn't just us."

"Where was this party?"

"Over where she live', over to the Coliseum. Like, all of the Head Nurses have these parties. They invite the staff and they friends too."

"Yeah, I follow you."

"Well, they axed me if I could work the evening shif' that day 'cause they was short. So I work' seven-to-three, and then I work' three-to-eleven. You know?"

I nodded.

"So I don't get there till almost midnight. And as soon as I come in I knowed I made a mistake."

"Why?"

"'Cause all the other staff already been there and gone. That's what I'm telling you about these parties. If it ain't no hospital party, and you' just a worker from the unit, they expects you to stay for a little while, and then leave."

"Nice system."

"Now, I don't mean it was no racial thing. It was the *employees* I'm talkin' about."

"I understand. It still stinks. What happened?"

"Well, there I am, see, and I still got my uniform on, and everybody else there is these Residents and Interns and they girlfriends. They all smokin' weed, and they got the lights turned down. I'm gonna leave, but then this medical student hand' me a beer, so I'm gonna stay and drink it, you know. Then all this noise start' up in the bedroom."

"Noise?"

"Somebody yellin' *Right on!* and like that. An' everybody heard it, 'cause they start lookin' to see what's goin' on. And then somebody open' the door."

"And?"

Jackson looked embarrassed. "The first thing I seen is this Intern or whatever he was standin' there, and his pants is down around his shoes. He's got his back to the door, and his head's throwed back, and he's sayin' *Oh, baby* -- you know?"

"I get the picture."

"Then all the Interns and them starts up with, *Go! Go!* and like that. So he turns around to take a bow, like, an' everybody's laughin', and that's when I see it's Miss Gruber doin' him.

Jackson looked at me anxiously. I said, "So what happened then?"

"Well, she look up and she's lookin' me right in the face. I mean, she seen me, and she know' I seen her. So I turn aroun' and leave right away. I go home, an' I don' even say nothing about it to my wife."

We sat there for a while, breathing in the glue-fumes and squirming a little at the unexpected intimacy that Jackson's story had conjured up between us. He crumpled his lunch-bag into a ball. I said, "Did Joyce ever say anything to you…"

Jackson shook his head. "Nex' Monday it's go-to-work like usual. But then she start gettin' on me. She keep writin' me these memos about how bad my work goin'. I don't pay no attention. But then one day she tell me I'm fired. My wife tell' me to go down to Personnel, but they don't know nothin' down there. I can't tell them about no party."

"You should have. You might not be here."

We sat there and looked at the dingy walls for a while. It was nearly twelve-thirty. Jackson said, "What she done now that you investigatin'?"

"I don't know yet. Maybe nothing. I appreciate you telling me this."

Jackson wadded up his lunch-bag. "I ain't got much to lose, do I?"

We walked back to the room where the other employees were watching the time-clock tick its way toward twelve-thirty. The attractive woman with no teeth was talking with a beefy white man in a brown leisure suit and a ridiculous-colored shirt. She was asking him if they could bring in a record player to play Christmas music on their breaks. "We don't want to play no dance music, Mr. Walsh." Everybody laughed. She said, "You ought to come out dancin' with us sometime, Mr. Walsh. You know how to *Shake Your Bootie?*"

The beefy man stared at the wall and said, "I can do that,"

"You never did give us no answer about our record player, sir."

Walsh pulled the corners of his mouth up into a smug little grin. "No, I didn't. And I'm not going to, either." He strutted off through a door and into some kind of office.

Jackson and I exchanged glances. I said, "Don't give up yet," and got out of there as fast as I could.

Chapter 6

I drove back to the hospital and found another parking space that overlooked the construction site. I was hungry, but I didn't want to go into the building and fish around blindly. I watched a mixer-truck gush concrete into a wooden form. Joyce Gruber, Miss Deep Throat of Riverview Hospital. There were a lot of oral-sex references in the letters, but that didn't prove anything in particular. And the party had happened six months before Barry Alspach had set foot in town.

    I dug the typing samples out of the glove compartment again. Maybe if I looked at them long enough I'd integrate with the karma of the writer. Or maybe I'd just get crosseyed. I looked at the other side of the yellow sheet that I'd torn off the pad on Barry's desk. Handwritten, it read:

> *DS - guild mentality in MR*
> *duplic effort / must handcopy*
> *Lookup statutes, AHA guidelines, MRL ditto*

The rest of the page was a list of titles and page numbers, including citations for the Ohio Revised Code. It didn't sound like it had anything to do with disposable equipment or autoclaving.

My stomach began to churn again. I pocketed the samples and walked back through the garage and the hospital to the cafeteria. It was after one o'clock, and the crowd was thin. I loaded up with runny-looking beans and franks. There was no way they could screw up a hot dog. I paid the cashier and looked around for a place to sit.

Darlene Kotecki and another girl were sitting at a table with two empty seats. When I caught her eye, she looked down at her plate. I hadn't had an invitation that friendly since I applied for a small-business loan. I walked over to the table and sat down.

She looked at me like I was going to hit her. I said, "Hello, Miss Kotecki," as politely as I could without a bow and a flourish. It always seemed to work for Peter Lawford, but it never got me anywhere. I looked at her friend. She was a skinny little thing in a nurse's uniform and short-cropped white-blonde hair. Her lips were pursed as tightly as Darlene's. Her badge said *C. Leeds LPN.*

I introduced myself and asked her what her name was. She croaked, "Cathy," in the smallest voice possible. She and Darlene looked like a pair of terrified white mice.

I munched down a few forkfuls of beans and said, "Do you two work together?"

Darlene said, "No. I'm on Seven South."

As a scintillating luncheon, this one was going to be a flop. I thought about asking Darlene how Parker was feeling, but I decided against it. I was trying to think of something useful to snoop about when Darlene announced, "We have to get back to work, Mr. Chandler." They both stood up and carried their trays across the room without moving a muscle that wasn't absolutely necessary. They were a pair of nervous breakdowns looking for a place to happen.

I finished the beans and sipped glumly on my iced tea. I wished that Joan would pop in for lunch, but she didn't. There were two wall-phones in the cafeteria. I went to the nearest one, dialed the operator, and asked for Siehl's office. She told me that it was 383, and that I could dial it myself.

Joan answered the phone, and I said, "You ought to give voice lessons, you know."

"Frank! Are you back already?"

"Yes. Oliver Jackson was a dead end. Is Siehl there?"

"Yes, he is. I'll switch you."

"Wait a minute. Can you find out the name of the LPN who complained about Joyce Gruber?"

"Sure. I mean I'll try to."

"Why don't you find out and then come down here to the cafeteria with me. I'm all lonesome and blue."

"Hold on a minute. Yes, Mr. Siehl?"

I heard Siehl's bossy voice saying something in the background. I said, "See you later," and hung up. I hurried out of the cafeteria, up the stairs, and across the lobby into the administrative suite. I barged into Siehl's office while he was still talking to Joan. She still had the phone in her hand. He finished saying something about airline tickets and looked at me like a stain on the rug. He said, "I hope you've got my four hundred dollars."

"I gave it to the Lydia Pinkham Foundation." He just scowled harder. I said, "I told you that I'd send it to you on Friday, and I will. Right now I've got more important things to worry about."

"Like what?"

"Like a 'guild mentality.'"

He blinked and stared at me as though I'd pulled a pigeon out of my pocket. *Bingo*. I said, "Can we talk?"

He looked at me dubiously. "Come in here."

We walked into his office, and Siehl shut the door behind him. I sank down in one of his chairs and tried not to look too eager. For the first time that I'd seen, Siehl seemed embarrassed. He said, "Okay. When did you talk to Barry and what did he tell you?"

"I never talked to him. I saw some notes he made from a conversation with you. It looked like you two were working on a project. What was it?"

"Son of a bitch." He looked like I'd caught him stealing the poorbox. I watched him stew and fume. Finally he said, "I hope to Christ I wasn't pushing him too hard."

"Nobody's blaming you for anything. But the

police are investigating Barry's death, and you'd better have your story straight if they start asking questions."

That was about as likely as a free lunch, but it didn't matter. Siehl came out from behind his desk and sat down in a chair beside me. He lit a cigarette and puffed on it repeatedly to get it started. He said, "Barry came to me. I want you to remember that." I nodded. He said, "It was around the first of November. He came in here and sat right there where you're sitting. He was really discouraged. He talked for a long time about how much this internship meant to him, and how he wanted to get his career off to a good start, and that kind of thing. You know?"

"I follow you."

"So then he started telling me about this horseshit project that George Gibbs had assigned to him. You remember I was telling you about George Gibbs? Well, this was typical. He'd assigned Barry to piss around with questions like whether to let the patients keep their thermometers or to wipe them off and put them back in the drawer. I mean, we use maybe three hundred dollars' worth of thermometers a year, but the budget for this place is around twenty million, and three hundred dollars doesn't amount to a fart in a windstorm. You see what I mean?"

"Okay. It was a lousy assignment. Did you send him back to straighten it out with Gibbs?"

Siehl began to get angry. "George Gibbs wouldn't know a good idea if it bit him on the ass." He mashed out his cigarette and lit another. Banker's butts. After he puffed on it a few times, he said, "So I told him that I'd help him work out his internship. See, Barry came here from George Washington University, and that's where I got my degree. I told him that I'd call up the faculty, because I keep in pretty close touch with those people, you know? See, hospital administration is really a pretty small world."

"I can see that."

"So I told him that what he needed was a really good project that he could develop into a thesis when he applied for a fellowship with the College of Hospital Administrators. And Barry said that he wanted to do that. I mean it was his choice."

"What was the topic?"

Siehl took a long drag and exhaled it slowly. "Computerizing medical records."

We sat there in silence for a few seconds. The cigarette smoke eddied around the ceiling. Finally I said, "So what?"

Siehl looked at me incredulously. "'So *what?*'"

"It sounds like the most logical thing in the world to do. What's the big deal?"

He took a deep breath and said, "Look. The medical records system is a huge pain in the ass. We have a computer here that could do ninety per cent of the work. Like if somebody's in here to get their ulcers X-rayed, the computer can order the barium shit that you drink, tell Dietary to hold the breakfast, call Transportation, and add the charges to the bill. But the god-damn medical records have to be handwritten. There are state laws and national AHA guidelines, and the medical records people have their own axe to grind."

"Or a 'guild mentality?'"

"Yeah. So I told Barry to do a study. He could have pointed the way to turn the whole thing around."

The intercom buzzed, and Siehl went over to his desk and picked up the phone. He said, "Yes, Mr. Ross," and got absorbed in scribbling notes and repeating, "Uh-huh. Uh-huh." I tried to make connections between computerized medical records and suicides. Maybe one of the medical records librarians had threatened to beat him to death with a ball-point pen.

Siehl hung up the phone and looked at me blankly. I said, "One thing is for sure. Barry didn't kill himself because you overworked him. I don't understand why you had to be so damn devious about it, though."

"Oh, hell. That's just the way this place works." He nodded at the telephone. "That was Ross just now. He shot down my proposal to expand the vending-machine area and make it an employee lunchroom for the night shift. He claims that it's a security risk, you know? That's bullshit. That's George Gibbs's favorite argument against everything, and it means that George sabotaged me on this one. But I've got him set up for things he hasn't even thought of yet."

"Ross must think he's okay."

Siehl looked at me with utter contempt. "Ross?

You know what Ross is? He's a piddookey-bird. You know what a piddookey-bird is?"

"Tell me."

"A piddookey-bird is a bird that flies in decreasing circles until it finally flies up its own asshole. That's Ross."

I looked around Siehl's fancy office again. It would take me six months to buy his furniture if I didn't eat or pay rent. I said, "Let's get back to this medical records business. Who did Barry talk to on this project?"

"Hell, I don't know. Medical Records Librarians and Ward Clerks."

"Ward Clerks?"

"Yeah. They enter a lot of stuff in the records."

"What's in a medical record?"

"Oh, hell. It's a whole package, and it's different depending on what you're in for. The doctors dictate their notes. There's the admission sheet, and the nursing notes, and the kardex, and the pharmaceutical..."

"What's a kardex?"

"Oh, it's a summary of treatment information and nursing activities and stuff. Why?"

I said, "You've just made my day. Thanks." I left Siehl standing behind his desk hollering, "Now, wait a goddamned minute!" It would do him good to feel left out for a while.

In the outer office, Joan said, "I've got a present for you." She handed me a three-by-five card. On it was printed *Catherine Leeds, LPN. 828 Wheeler*

Street, Apartment 3.

I said, "How about drinks and dinner?"

"How about just drinks. Tomorrow after work."

"My place or yours?"

"I think we'd better go to the Vickers Hotel bar."

"Swell. I'll brush up on my Gertrude Lawrence numbers."

"Wouldn't Cole Porter be more your style? Or is there something you aren't telling me?"

"As long as you're with me, I don't think anybody's going to doubt my proclivities. I'll be the envy of the neighborhood. See you!" I took off feeling like a stallion in springtime.

Chapter 7

Cathy Leeds's apartment reminded me uncomfortably of Barry Alspach's. Somebody was squeezing out a lot of rent without providing a nickel's worth of maintenance. I'd positioned my car across the street at two-thirty, but at four she still hadn't come home. The longer I sat there, the less sure I felt about the pattern that I'd glimpsed in Siehl's office. Barry had contacted Joyce Gruber through his medical records investigation. Cathy Leeds worked for Joyce. Cathy was a friend of Darlene Kotecki. But at Riverview Hospital everybody worked haunch-to-paunch with everybody else. Maybe Cathy had screwed Barry. Maybe Darlene had screwed Barry. Maybe Cathy had screwed Darlene.

I carried around a copy of *Gravity's Rainbow* for stake-outs and other empty moments. I could read it in fits and starts without losing the thread, if there was one. I stared at the pages for a while, but I couldn't concentrate. I kept thinking about Cathy Leeds's white-blonde hair. It looked like she'd dyed it to match Darlene's. Sometimes insecure girls like Cathy would attach themselves desperately to flashier girls like Darlene. Cathy could be jealous as hell of Darlene's time and attention. Maybe jealous enough to write poison-pen letters to Darlene's boyfriend.

I liked it better and better. I wondered if Cathy had been working for Joyce Gruber when Joyce dated Richard Parker. I wondered if she had tried to be Joyce's twin the same way she was trying to be Darlene's.

I was wondering whether Cathy had ever gone out with Barry Alspach when she drove up and parked across the street. Her car was a Rabbit. I wasn't surprised. She walked around to the passenger-door, lifted a bag of groceries off the seat, and trudged up the sidewalk with a wobbly gait. Her legs looked frail as toothpicks under the white nurse's stockings. As soon as she got through the outside door of the apartment, I bailed out of the car and hustled in after her.

I caught up with her while she was standing in front of her apartment door trying to get her key in the keyhole while holding the groceries with one arm. I said, "Here, let me help you," and lifted the bag away from her. She didn't know whether to be alarmed or relieved. I gave her my most innocuous smile, which just rattled her more. I said, "You remember me, don't you? We met today at lunch..."

"I know who you are." She said it so fast that all

the words ran together. She got the door open and then looked worriedly at the grocery-bag in my arms. I said, "Gee, you've got a lot of heavy stuff in here," and I walked past her into her apartment. It looked like a transplanted dormitory room. There were Snoopy posters and Walter Keane prints on the walls. On an end-table she had one of those stretched-out Pepsi bottles with the stem of a big paper flower stuck in it. I carried the groceries into the kitchenette. There were enough dirty cups in the sink to stock a tea-shop. An aging sackful of garbage put off a throat-closing smell. There was also a penetrating stink of cat litter.

I went back into the living room, where Cathy was still standing beside the door. She started to say, "Thank you for bringing in the groceries, but I think you'd better..."

"You're welcome. Miss Leeds, may I ask you a personal question?"

She flinched as though I'd thrown something at her. "Look, I really have a lot to do..."

"Did you know Barry Alspach?"

"Who?" She looked relieved. She must have thought I was going to rape her on the rug.

"He was the Administrative Intern at Riverview. He killed himself yesterday."

"Oh, I heard somebody killed themself."

"But you know who I'm talking about."

"No, I don't. I mean, I think I saw him at the hospital. But I don't know very many people, really. Specially from the Administration."

Specially. Yes. I knew what had been bothering me about the letters. I also knew that Cathy was telling the truth about not knowing many people. She was the loneliest, most frightened girl I'd seen in a long time.

A gray Siamese cat darted out from under a chair and ran into the hall. Cathy wailed, "Oh, Sam!" and started to chase him. I hotfooted behind. I passed Cathy as the cat started to bound up the stairs to the second floor, and I stamped up the steps as hard as I could. The noise startled the cat, and he froze. I nabbed him on the landing. He went limp and looked at me with innocent blue-gray eyes.

I handed the cat back to Cathy, and she hugged him. We walked back down the hall to her apartment. I followed her in again, and she didn't seem to mind. I said, "By the way, do you have a typewriter?"

She was still holding the cat. "No."

"Do you know how to type?"

"No, I don't. Why..."

"Why did you complain about having your schedule shifted around?"

She began to glance around wildly. I looked at her and the cat. I looked at the Walter Keane pictures with their teardrops and big, sad eyes. I felt like a tax-collector in a poorhouse. I said, "There's some dirty, stinking business going on at Riverview Hospital. I'm going to find out what it is. I think that Darlene Kotecki is involved in it, and I think Joyce Gruber is involved in it, and I think you're involved in it."

She looked like I'd kicked her in the stomach. Her chin was trembling, and she was ready to cry. I shouted, "I'm tired of these goddamned games! You can lie and try to hide it till hell freezes over..."

She screamed, *"No!"* and threw the cat into a chair. She ran around me and out the door. The cat made another jailbreak and took off like a shot down the hall. I heard the front door bang shut, and I walked over to her window. Cathy ran across the front yard, climbed in her car, and dug frantically in her pockets for keys. She started the car and took off so wildly that a Buick coming down the street had to slam on its brakes and pull over to give her a wide berth.

I looked in her bathroom and bedroom, and then in all the closets and kitchen cabinets. She really didn't have a typewriter. She didn't have much of anything else, either. I went back down the hall and up the stairs where the cat was waiting to play more hide-and-seek. He purred loudly while I carried him back to Cathy's apartment. I chucked him inside and closed the door. Then I got out of there before she came to her senses and called the police.

I drove back to my office and looked in to check for mail. There wasn't any. The broken bookcase had disappeared from the hall. Otherwise nothing had changed, nothing at all. I wished that someone would steal my old magazines or bring me some new ones.

I drove home and found a parking space in front of my apartment. Wonders would never cease. I walked up the street to the grocery store and bought frozen shrimp and a bottle of chardonnay. I found myself hurrying back to the apartment. Cathy Leeds was hooked into this business. I hoped I'd scared her enough to make the next shoe drop.

I moved the phone into the kitchen. I had a fine old time melting butter and making the wine sauce. I was tearing up spinach leaves for a salad when the phone rang. *Joyce, baby,* I thought, *your chickens have come home to roost.*

I picked up the phone and said, "Hello."

"How'd you like to go through life in a wheelchair, Chief?"

"Well, Pretty Boy Floyd. Your fingers still sore?"

"You got shit in your ears, man? I tol' you to butt out."

"Where do you fit into all this?"

He was quiet for a minute. Then he said, "It ain't nothin' but somethin' to do. Keep your ears open, Chief." He hung up.

I sat and listened to the quiet bubbling of the wine-sauce in the oven. I could hear the hum of traffic from Columbia Parkway half a mile away. Nobody could shoot into my apartment without a helicopter or a hook-and-ladder. The only way to cause any real damage was to set the place on fire. I wondered if he was crazy enough to try.

I decided to-hell-with-it and went back into the kitchen. I finished the salad and dug some frozen fancy vegetables out of the refrigerator. I put a pan of water on the stove to boil. It was a quarter to seven. Outside it looked cold and dark as Finland.

There was a roar like a bomb and a screech of tires in the street. I was through the front door and down the steps three at a time. Outside there was a smell of exhaust fumes and cordite. The air was cold and clammy. Nobody was face-down on the sidewalk.

I stepped out into the street. There was a black smudge on the left front quarter-panel of the Fairlane, and a finger-sized hole in the middle of the smudge. I looked under the car. Water and antifreeze and oil were dribbling out on the pavement.

I looked up and down the street. Nobody was in a hurry to run out to see what happened. The faces behind the windows looked pasty and scared. I didn't blame them. Somebody hollered *What's going on?* I went back inside.

I turned off the oven and put all the food back into the refrigerator. Then I went into the bedroom and pulled out the safe from the back of the closet. It wasn't much of a safe, but it was a little too big for the cleaning lady to carry away. I dialed the combination, and it clicked open on the first try. I set the Konika and lenses aside, along with the envelopes of the insurance policies and a few first-day-of-issue stamps. I lifted out the bundle at the bottom, slipped off the plastic cover, and unwrapped the oilcloth from the Browning nine-millimeter. The two clips were full. I slipped one into the butt of the handle and put the other in my pocket.

My shoulder-holster was under a pile of

sweaters in a dresser-drawer. I slipped it on and secured the pistol in it with the leather strap. I knew that the safety was on and that there were no bullets in the chamber, but I still didn't like to carry the damn thing. I put on a tweed sportcoat to hide it. The bulge looked obvious as a pocket full of marbles. *Like a tumor,* Robert Penn Warren had written. I got out my car-coat and put that on, too. The bulge didn't show. It would be hell to pay in a fast-draw contest, but I didn't plan to get into one.

I phoned a cab company and walked outside to wait. There was a steady rivulet of oil and water running from under my car down the gutter and into the storm sewer. Two guys in polyester suits and stylish topcoats were standing in the street admiring the hole in the fender and telling each other that Dirty Harry used one of those guns in the movies. I didn't bother to correct them. The cab rolled up, and I was glad to get away before the police came nosing around.

The driver was a twenty-five-year-old kid with a beard. There wasn't enough knee-room in the back seat. I scootched around sideways and said, "Newport."

The driver raised his eyebrows in mock irony. "Any particular place?"

"The *Mon Cheri.*"

"Ah, the *Moanin' Cherry.* Yes, sir."

He made a few more sorties at conversation, but I ignored him. We circled down from Mount Adams and into a dark warehouse-and-factory area that was criss-crossed with railroad tracks. We crossed the river on the new interstate-highway bridge that was waiting patiently for the freeways to link up with it on both ends. There were potholes as soon as we got off the bridge on the Kentucky side. We passed two liquor stores with fancy neon beacons and smaller printed signs that said *No Drinking in Parking Lot.* Cigarette butts glowed in the cars alongside the buildings.

We turned up York Street and passed the burned-out remains of the Pink Pussycat Go-Go Bar. The man who'd owned the place had been gunned down a year before the fire. They'd also torched a large, fancy supper club called the Lookout House. It was a nice neighborhood if you could temper your greed with obedience.

The *Mon Cheri* had a heart-shaped neon sign that needed a good cleaning and some fresh paint. The driver leered at me in comeradely fashion while I paid the fare. He said, "They sure know how to have a good time over here."

"Yeah, if you like the tinkle of broken promises."

A brass-plated mama at the door charged me two dollars to get in. The bar was dark and loud as the inside of a jukebox. Four girls in tacky spangled bikinis were sitting at a table at the far end. Dimly visible on the wall were cartoon murals of Parisian street cafes, the Eiffel tower, a pissoir, and lots of busty apache women. Lewd cartoonists had started suggesting nipples on their oversized breasts in the last few years. Things were looking up.

It was eight o'clock, and I was the only customer in the place. I sat at the bar and ordered a beer. The bartender was a hulking kid with a wide, expressionless face and hooded eyes. While he was setting the bottle and a glass on the bar, one of the girls drifted up out of the gloom and sat on the next stool. She had acne-scars under her makeup. She put her hand on my thigh and said, "Would you like some company? I'm Lori."

"Sister, I know too many people already."

She looked at the bartender with a helpless expression, and he glowered at me. I said to him, "I want to talk to Korte."

"Who?" He looked at me like a wax dummy on display.

"Tell him it's Chandler, from across the river."

"I dunno what you mean." He pretended to straighten some glasses that were drying on a green rubber mat.

"The hell you don't. He owns this place, and half the street. You can check it out, have them send somebody over here, or be as cagey as you want. But I'm going to sit here until I talk to Korte."

He shrugged and wandered down to the other end of the bar, feigning boredom. The girl evaporated off the stool and huddled with the others at the far table. Nobody came back to offer me another thigh-squeeze.

The disco music kept blaring. Two teenage boys tried to get in the door, but Big Mama turned them away. I looked around to see if the bartender was still dusting off the salted peanuts, but he had disappeared. There was a curious-looking beer can on the bar. I picked it up, and it rattled. It had started life as a real beer can, but somebody had put some pebbles inside and welded a new top on it. There were bar-napkin jokes and cartoons on the sides. A big-breasted girl was holding a pair of stockings, one in each hand, labeled *Merry Christmas* and *Happy New Year*. The pop-eyed fellow next to her was saying, "Mind if I come up between the holidays?" There were other cans on all the tables. Something for the customers to horse around with during the go-go routines.

I was trying to decide if rattling a can of rocks at a go-go dancer was a sexual activity between consenting adults when the bartender appeared and motioned for me to come to the end of the bar. He was standing in the doorway of a butler's pantry full of liquor bottles. A phone and an adding machine sat on a small white table alongside a cigar box full of receipts. The place was lit by a forty-watt bulb. The phone was off the hook. I stepped in and picked it up, and the bartender closed the door behind me. I said, "Korte?"

"What the hell is it, Chandler?" I could hear a television in the background. Music and dancing.

"What's your interest in Riverview Hospital?"

A few seconds went by. He said, "I don't appreciate when people call me just to fuck around."

"If I wanted to fuck around, I wouldn't do it with you. I don't care what you're doing at Riverview.

I just need to know if you're doing anything."

Korte exhaled loudly. "I got my gall bladder took out there two-three years ago. I ain't seen the place since. Why?"

"Because a guy who I think works for you keeps trying to chase me away from there. He's a big cowboy with a magnum. He blew a hole in my engine block tonight."

"Where?"

"Across the river. In front of my apartment."

"Son of a bitch. What's the guy look like?"

"He's about six-five and looks like Joe Namath. Dresses like a French whore."

He coughed and cleared his throat twice. He didn't sound too good. "Shame about your car. Maybe I could fix you up with a new one, cheap."

"Thanks but no thanks. I'd hate to try to register it. But I'd appreciate it if you'd get that hot-shot off my back."

"You're all right, Chandler. You're dumb, but you're all right."

"Give me a number where I can reach you."

"No chance. You can get me if you need me bad enough." He hung up.

I sat there among the gloom and liquor-bottles. The blatting music from the bar was muffled to the point of tolerability. The closet made a good phone booth. I dialed Joyce Gruber's number. It rang ten times before I hung up.

I opened the door and stepped back into the gaudy darkness of the bar. A couple of nervous-looking guys had come in and were sitting at a table. Two of the girls were sitting beside them with big fixed smiles, dolloping champagne out of a bottle as fast as they could drink it. That was going to set somebody back twenty dollars or so. One of the other girls was frugging half-heartedly on a platform with a mirror behind it. I said, "Thanks," to the bartender on my way to the door. He looked at me like an utter stranger.

Outside a cold rain was on the verge of turning to ice. Sin City looked about as exciting as Newark, New Jersey. I hailed a cab. The old geezer who drove me home had been around that part of town long enough to learn how to keep his questions to himself.

Chapter 8

The next morning I called used-car dealerships until I found one with an old brown Impala on the lot. I rode over in a cab and wandered around by myself before the salesman came out and started shepherding me. I was pleased to find that it was hard to spot the Impala in the crowd. The salesman got edgy when I asked him to start it up and stamp on the gas pedal. The smoke that came out of the tailpipe was mild compared to the pall that the Fair lane had produced. Chandler, the one-man ecological disaster. I test-drove the car through every rut and chuckhole I could find, and when I was satisfied that the heater worked and the wheels weren't going to fall off, I bought it.

I got to the hospital at noon. Joan was wearing a gorgeous maroon sweater and all kinds of fancy wire necklaces. I couldn't tell if she'd put on some fancy come-hither eye makeup or if she just sparkled naturally.

I said, "You look better than Paulette Goddard."

She pretended to be miffed, "Well, I hope so. She's about eighty."

"Yeah, but when she was with Charlie Chaplin, she was gorgeous. Where's Siehl?"

"He's out to lunch with Dr. Parker. As a matter of fact, I was about to go down to the cafeteria myself. Care to join me?"

"If we go to lunch, it's not going to be in the cafeteria. But I'm so damned wound-up that I couldn't stop to eat now if I wanted to. Where can I find Joyce Gruber?"

She looked at me with those eyes again. "What are you so wound-up about?"

"You. And a problem that I think I can crack before we go drinking this afternoon. Where's Joyce?"

"Well, if those are your priorities, I guess I'll call the Nursing Office."

While she was dialing and talking on the phone, I noticed a picture behind the coat-rack that I hadn't seen before. It was a detailed, Gustave-Dore-styled etching of Sisyphus shouldering his rock up the hill. I could only see half of it behind the coats and hangers. When Joan hung up, I said, "Who put this back here?"

"You know, that's Mr. Siehl's favorite picture. Mr. Ross made the administrators hang those Sierra Club photographs in their offices because he thought it would be good for the hospital's image, so Mr. Siehl put that out here. Anyway, Joyce isn't here today."

"Why?"

"She called in sick this morning. Do you want her address?"

"I already have it."

She looked at me coolly. "You already have it?"

"Doesn't everybody? It's strictly business, and I'm afraid that before this is over I'll wish I'd never heard of her. Remember what you said about turning people in?"

"You think it's her, then?"

"If it's not her, I'll bet she knows who it is." A little pall of gloom was beginning to settle around us, I said, "I'll meet you at the Vickers Hotel at five o'clock." She didn't respond at all. I said, "Is something the matter?"

"I wish I knew how I felt right now. It's really strange. You're going to confront Joyce now, I suppose. Then what?"

"Who knows? Maybe I'll turn her in. Maybe I'll give her Parker's money and tell her to split for California. See you at five." I left to shut off the discussion. I really didn't know what I was going to do.

Joyce lived in the Coliseum Apartments, a variegated complex of high-rises and tennis courts and swimming pools. Singles only. I parked the car and walked from building to building until I picked out the tower that was Joyce's address. There were two walls of mailboxes in the lobby, plus two cigarette machines and a pay phone. Candy wrappers and cigarette butts had been kicked into the corners and left there. There wasn't any guard.

I dropped a dime in the phone and dialed Joyce's number. It rang ten times, and I hung up. I checked the mailboxes and found that her apartment was eight-twenty-two. I rode the elevator to her floor, sharing part of the ride with an old woman and a mop bucket.

The hall was empty. I walked to her door and banged on it for a while. There wasn't any answer, and I didn't expect one. The door was well-hung, fitting tightly into the frame. The plastic strip in my wallet wouldn't work worth a damn. What I needed was a good Cuban locksmith.

There was a peephole in the door with a fisheye lens in it. From inside you'd be able to see both ends of the hall in a widely-distorted arc. You could damn near see the back of your head with one of those things. From the outside you could only see a point of light in the glass. I wondered if you could line up a few lenses in a tube and see into an apartment from the hall side. I put my eye up to the lens. It looked like a bright dot of light with a greenish tinge.

I didn't have lenses or locksmiths or a battering-ram. I didn't have anything except a strong hunch that there was a typewriter in Joyce's apartment that had been used to dispatch a lot of venom. In the movies you could always seduce the chambermaid and snatch her keys. In the Coliseum Apartments you could only cool your heels in the hall like a disappointed suitor.

I had given up breaking-and-entering and was

ready to go back to the hospital to lean harder on Cathy Leeds when the point of light in Joyce's peephole blinked off and on again. Somebody was in there. I started knocking slowly and steadily. While I kept up the tattoo with one hand, I fished out my wallet, slipped out a business card, and wrote ME OR THE POLICE on the back. To hell with grammar. I slipped it under the door and kept knocking. A full minute went by, and I hoped that the neighbors wouldn't start sticking their heads out in the hall. They didn't. Finally a safety-chain rattled and clacked loose on the inside, and a very small strangled-sounding female voice said, "Come in."

I stepped inside and shut the door. There was a very short hall that led to a living room. To the right was a kitchenette. Nobody was in there. Three feet ahead was the living room. There was a sliding glass door that led out to a balcony on the other side of the room. That was where the light in the peephole had come from. There was a handful of completely conventional furniture and a green rug. Through an open doorway I could see a cluttered bedroom and an unmade bed. Oliver Jackson would have had a perfect view from where I stood.

Joyce was standing in the middle of the living room. She was wearing blue jeans and a work shirt, and she stood like someone who had been kicked in the guts. Her hands were clasped together in front of her stomach, and it took a few seconds to see the tiny muzzle of a gun pointing at me. It was a .22 pistol not much bigger than a roll of scotch tape. Joyce looked wretched. The whites showed all around her eyes, and she was trembling. She said, "You're going to sit down and wait until Eddie gets back."

"Eddie who?"

She pointed the gun at my face, and I hoped fervently that it had a stiff trigger. "Stay away from me!"

"If you hit somebody with that thing, they're likely to get mad and take it away from you."

She hunched her shoulders even further. She was ready for a good case of hysterics. "Sit down!"

I said, "I *am* going to sit down, and I think that you should, too. I'm not going to hurt you unless you do something dumb like shooting at me. And that won't accomplish anything except get you in a bigger mess than you're in already." I lowered myself into a wood-and-canvas sling chair.

Joyce looked like she hadn't slept for a week. She looked like she needed a hug and some reassurance, but that could wait until she put the gun down. She stepped back and sat on the edge of the black leather sofa. I tried to keep looking at her eyes instead of the gun.

We sat there for ages and listened to the refrigerator hum. I finally said, "You can't lose anything by talking to me. Nobody's going to punish you if you just get your head together and stop the harassment."

In spite of her fear and suspicion, she looked surprised. "What in the world are you talking about?"

"Isn't it time to stop playing games..."

"No! I'm not playing games. What are you talking about?"

I said, "The letters."

"What letters?"

I believed her. She really didn't know. And I'd hounded her and her friends half to death. I stood up and walked to the glass doors that led to the balcony. She made a little noise, but she didn't shoot me. I looked out at the bleak vista of parking lots and brick buildings. I said, "Miss Gruber, something crazy as hell is going on. A man you used to know is being harassed with poison-pen letters and phone calls. Last night somebody blew a hole in my car with a magnum revolver. And now you're sitting here pointing a gun at me. Why?"

She looked down at the gun in her hands. She pointed it away from me, but she didn't put it down. She said, "That isn't what you told me the other day in the cafeteria."

"What did you think I told you?"

"You said that the boy who killed himself had found out something. And then yesterday you accused Cathy Leeds of being involved."

"That's right. And she nearly fell apart at the seams. I believe that you didn't write the letters. But you've done something that you're damn worried that I'll discover."

Her face pinched into a knot of pain. "You don't know what it's like. I'm thirty-eight years old, and I don't have anybody. *Anybody.*"

"You're not the only one in that boat." She didn't hear me. I was damned if I was going to play Miss Lonelyhearts for Joyce. People only fumbled around and then they could never find the words. Maybe there weren't any. I said, "At least you're able to get up on your hind legs and laugh and cry and point guns at people. Barry Alspach's never going to be thirty-eight."

She sighed deeply. "So what do you want?"

"I want to know what a nice decent kid might have stumbled over that would make him want to kill himself."

She stared blankly at some point over my shoulder that only she could see. "This is insane. I don't know you at all. You shouldn't even be here."

"I know. I'm an inconvenient bastard. But there's one big difference between me and the police. They have to write down everything you say and turn it over to the County Prosecutor. That's like handing a wounded rabbit to a sick wolf. He bites, you're gone, and he's licking his chops for the next kill. And we actually pay that son of a bitch to do that. But if I get there first, I can choose to keep it to myself. And I don't like to see people get hurt."

She said, "Oh, dear God," and she looked down at the pistol in her hands. For a terrible few seconds I wondered if she was going to point it at me or at herself. Then she laid it gingerly on the coffee table, like a teacup in an antique shop. She pulled a wadded-up Kleenex out of her pants pocket and blew her nose. She said, "All right," and shuddered and blew her nose again.

I sat back down in the chair, and she perched on the edge of the sofa. I said, "So what's this all about?"

Joyce fumbled for a place to start. "Oh, it was silly, really. I mean it started out that way. Cathy's an LPN, and she worked for me on the Recovery Unit. She was okay, you know. I mean she really tried hard, but she wasn't very well-oriented in her procedures. It doesn't take that much training to be an LPN."

I nodded to show that I was listening, and she went on. "But then last summer Cathy made friends with – with a Ward Clerk. And she became very ineffective. She was always taking long lunch hours and a lot of breaks and even going over to the other unit to see her friend. I really had to watch her."

"Do you think it was a lesbian arrangement?"

"No, I just don't think that Cathy was very strong. I think she just... Well, she just *worshipped* Darlene." She wrinkled her nose to show what she thought of Darlene, and then she realized that she'd mentioned her name. I said, "I know who you're talking about. Go ahead."

"Well, eventually she became so – so unreliable that I felt she needed to be transferred to a different shift." The Head Nurse in Joyce was beginning to show through. I wondered if Cathy had been unreliable, or if she had simply become a reminder that Richard Parker was dating Darlene. I didn't say anything. Joyce said, "So I transferred her to nights. You know, eleven-to-seven. That was when she complained to Personnel. They talked to me about it, but I told them that I felt it was best for the patients, and that was that."

She drew designs on the sofa with her forefinger while she talked. "That was in November. Well, about a week after I transferred her, the Charge Nurse on the night shift got sick. I had to fill in for her, because we're really short-staffed, you know? So it was just Cathy and me and one aide that night, but that was okay, because nothing much usually happens at night.

"But then about four a.m. there were two Code Blues. There were two patients..."

"What's a Code Blue?"

"It's a signal for the resuscitation team to come running. It usually means that somebody's going to die unless they get help."

"Okay. Go on."

"Oh, this is awful... Anyway, there were two patients down in Intensive Care who both had to be resuscitated at the same time. And then while that was going on, another heart attack came in through the Emergency Room. They needed an extra nurse in the ER, so they called me down from the floor. The unit was quiet, so I left Cathy in charge and told her to call me in the ER if she needed any help.

"So I went down to the ER and worked on the patient. He was real fat, and diabetic besides. We were down there for about an hour. Then in the middle of everything Cathy called me. She said that somebody had died on the unit, and she wanted me to come up and take care of it. Well, I couldn't leave the ER, so I told her to prep the body and get the paperwork ready, and I'd bring up the ER doctor as soon as I could.

"Well, it was another half-hour or so before we got the heart patient stabilized and up to Intensive Care. I went up to the unit with Dr. Wilcox, but they'd already shipped the body down to the morgue. He signed the death certificate and went back down to the ER. Cathy was real proud of herself because she thought she'd taken care of everything, but I thought I'd better check over the notes just to make sure."

Joyce looked up at me with a brittle smile. "You know what I found? She'd killed him."

I looked hard at her eyes for signs of a cock-and-bull story. "How did she do it?"

"Well, he was an old man, and he'd already had a stroke, and he must have had another in his sleep. The aide found him not breathing, and she told Cathy. Then Cathy called me and told me he was dead, so I told her to record the vital signs and prep the body. So she washed him down and packed his mouth and nose with cotton. Then she called Central Transportation and had them come and wheel him down to the morgue. But then in the notes she wrote that he had a heartbeat of ten."

"But you said the aide found him not breathing."

"She did. I asked her. But I guess the patient must have been doing Cheyne-Stokes breathing. That's where you breathe a few times, and then stop for a while. It can happen after a stroke. If she'd just sent the aide back to prep him... I mean, Mildred would have known what was going on. But Cathy just did what she was told."

"Why the business with the cotton?"

"That's just standard procedure with a corpse. You pack the anus, too."

I got up and looked out through the balcony doors again. The view hadn't improved a bit. I said, "So your Cathy crammed cotton into a patient's windpipe and killed him. What did you do?"

She said, "Well, I showed Cathy the notes and what she'd done, and she got panicky. I mean she cried and begged and pleaded with me not to report her. So I guess I got a little panicky, too. I sent her home and took care of the rest of the night by myself.

"And then the longer I sat there and thought about it, the more I was sure I'd get blamed. See, *I'd* transferred Cathy to nights, *I'd* left her alone, and I'd told her to prep the body. And whenever anything goes wrong at Riverview, they fire somebody. It doesn't make any difference how many people were involved, or why, as long as it's somebody's *fault*. Do you see what I'm saying?"

"It sounds familiar. Go ahead."

"Well, anyway, there are an awful lot of people who'd like to see me lose my job or get out of town. I know that sounds paranoid, but it's true. So after the shift was over in the morning I went to see Mr. Siehl."

"Why him?"

"Well, because he's different. He doesn't just try

to find blame and fire people."

"I wouldn't bet on it. What did he tell you?"

"He said to forget it. He said to make sure that the medical records were complete so that no one would look at them very carefully. So I did that, and he was right. I never heard another word about it.

"I transferred Cathy back to days where I could keep an eye on her. I had kind of forgotten about it, or I guess maybe I just wanted to, until you hit me with how Barry had killed himself because he found out something. I knew he was doing some kind of project with medical records, and that was the first thing I thought of. I guess... Now that I say it, it sounds..."

I looked around at her dime-store-danish furniture and her view of the parking lot. It wasn't my style, but she was trying to build some kind of home for herself. And not finding a lot of help along the way. I said, "I don't see that you intentionally hurt anybody. Or Cathy, either, for that matter. Some poor old bugger died, but it sounds like he was almost dead anyway. Have you told anyone else about this?"

"Well – no. Nobody at the hospital."

"Come on. Anybody at all?"

"Well – I told part of it to Eddie the other night. After you – after I saw you in the cafeteria."

"Is Eddie a big palooka who wears a lot of fancy clothes?"

She smiled a small ironic smile. "Do you know him?"

"Just tell him I'm not going to hurt you. He's

been trying to bring you my scalp for a souvenir." I started for the door, but I remembered a promise. "There's one more thing. You fired Oliver Jackson. Will you hire him back?"

"My God, how do you – what have you been doing to me?"

"Just nosing around. Will you hire him back?"

She sat ramrod-straight, biting her lip and starting to cry again. You could almost see the wall of loneliness and fear around her. I said, "I know that you manufactured the case to get him fired. You can have all that crap pulled out of his file. Will you do it?"

Her voice was so small I could barely hear her. "Yes. Of course."

I made one more feint at the door, but I stopped again. "Have you talked to Richard Parker lately?"

She looked shell-shocked. "Dick? What does he have to do with all this?"

I said, "Not a blessed thing," and left.

Chapter 9

Joan was waiting for me in the lobby of the Vickers Hotel. Two wrinkled-and-rouged old women in the overstuffed chairs were eyeing her enviously. They looked like they'd been sitting in hotel lobbies all their lives. Joan looked like the cover of *Vogue*. I said, "Buy you a drink, lady?"

She said, "You know, I used to see those William Powell movies on the late show, and I always wondered if anybody talked like him,"

"I think you've got your matinee idols mixed up. He was a lot more elegant than I'll ever be. Why did you wait out here?"

"Dave – Mr. Siehl's in the bar. I knew that if I went in by myself, he'd ask me to sit with him. I decided to wait for you. What's the matter?"

"Why do you ask?"

"Because you look rumpled, somehow. You look like you were in a race and your car broke down.

What happened with Joyce?"

"You should have been a psychiatrist. I'll tell you inside."

We walked together through the gray-glass door and into the gloom of the bar. There was a faint background wash of orchestral music, but no piano-player was on hand to attract the barflies. The waitress was stirring a metal chafing-dish full of Vienna sausages in a runny brown sauce. A sign behind the food and paper plates said *Happy Hour 4-7 Weekdays*. I said, "I've never been able to figure out why they call it *Happy*."

"You *are* a grump, aren't you? There's Mr. Siehl."

Siehl and Richard Parker were sitting in a booth. Neither of them looked excited about seeing us. I said, "'Evening,'" and started to walk by them when Parker said, "Have you got anything yet?"

"I told you I'd call you when I did."

"Think you could step it up a little?"

"You'll get your money's worth." Parker kept glowering. I said, "I'll call you tomorrow, Doctor," and I ushered Joan to a booth as far away from them as possible.

The waitress wandered by, and we ordered drinks. Joan said, "Well, what happened?"

"I've been sniffing up the wrong alley. It's a big fat zero. Joyce never wrote a smutty letter in her life."

"You know, I'm glad. I know who she is, and I feel kind of sorry for her."

"She's a mess, like everybody else. But she isn't

vindictive."

"I'll bet you're a lot of fun at parties. You're the most cynical man I've ever met. Why don't you take off your coat?"

"I don't want my gun to stick out."

She drew back a little. "Are you serious?"

"Yep. There's a big lug who shot up my car last night. He works for the Mob across the river, but he was trying to play knight-errant for a fair lady. I talked to his boss. He's going to be told to cool it, I don't think he's going to like it."

She ran her finger around the rim of her glass and stared into space. "You know, that's scary. You see it all the time on television, and you never think about it. But just sitting here talking with you, I have this image of a very insecure, irresponsible man with a gun who might shoot you. It seems wild and random, somehow,"

"He's not insecure. But he is trigger-happy." I wondered how hard Korte would crack down on him, but I knew I'd find out eventually. I looked across the room at Siehl and Parker in an animated conversation. "Didn't you tell me that those two had lunch together today?"

"They do that almost every day. I think that they're planning to take over the hospital."

"What do you mean?"

Joan smiled and said, "I probably shouldn't tell you."

"I shouldn't tell you that you're gorgeous. You shouldn't be out drinking with me. We shouldn't have fought in Vietnam. Tell me."

"Well, this is just based on what I've been able to pick up here and there. I think that the medical staff wants to get rid of Mr. Ross. They don't think he's very competent."

"Do you think he's competent?"

She looked surprised. "Thank you. Do you know how long it's been since anyone asked me- oh, never mind." She flicked the end of her swizzle-stick with one finger and stared at nothing in particular. I looked at the hollow of her throat and imagined what it would be like to kiss her there. Finally she said, "There's something wrong with this."

"Why? You don't need to have any loyalty..."

"No! That's not what I mean, and I'm not being a dewy-eyed Susie Secretary. *Competent* is the wrong word. It's one of those questions that slides away from the truth."

"Christ, lady, I think I love you. What's the right question?"

"He's not...*effective*. He's a paper man who's built a wall of paper around himself. I think that he must be terribly frightened. I worked at the hospital for three weeks before I even saw him."

"If he's such a milquetoast, how does he handle Siehl?"

She looked grim. "I hate to say this, but..."

"But what?"

"I'm afraid that Mr. Ross is going to fire him. He's had four Associate Administrators in seven years. I think that he must be threatened out of his mind by

Mr. Siehl."

I remembered what Joyce had said about people getting fired. "Does Siehl bad-mouth Ross when anybody will listen?"

She made a wry face. "I'm afraid so."

I took a pull on my drink. I looked at Siehl and Parker again. I said, "Have you ever wondered what the world would be like if everybody wasn't trying to stick a knife in everybody else's back?"

"Mmmmm. Do I detect a frustrated idealist?"

"Just another sorehead. Why are you working?"

She drew into herself a little. "It was just a personal decision. I just – I guess I wanted to see if I was still employable."

"Typing memos for Siehl is a funny way of proving anything. Is that all there is to it?"

She whipped around at me. "Don't you ever stop? You don't have to treat everybody like a criminal. What do you care, anyway?"

I said, "I'm a nosey bastard. It's painful for me, too. But I know that the questions you don't ask are the ones that bite you on the ass later on. And I like you."

She bit her lower lip. "I'm sorry. I didn't have to yell at you." We sat in silence for a while. Then she said, "I'm thinking of leaving my husband. I took this job... It was for money at first, to see if I could earn enough to support myself. What I've found out is that I can't. Do you know how much they pay?"

"I imagine damn little."

"There are women who've worked there for

years who still don't make eight thousand dollars."

"Then why are you still working? Why don't you go back to school?"

"I'm not sure I know why myself. I don't feel too sure about being able to handle school, either."

"Why are you leaving your husband?"

"Oh, he's – he's a salesman for Procter & Gamble, and all he likes to do is watch television. He watches all of those damn sports programs, and he knows all of their names and numbers and everything. When he plays with the boys, all he's interested in is winning. He's no *fun*. He's just – oh, I don't know."

"You have children?"

"Two boys."

We let a little silence roll by. The piano-player appeared from somewhere, and he began a quiet Lerner and Lowe medley. Joan said, "You know, I really like this. I enjoy being out and hearing some music and having drinks. If I were here with Bill, he'd be squirming around and miserable. Or else he'd be trying to show off and play the big spender." She started to say more, but she pressed her mouth shut.

I said, "I've never understood why the women I like get hooked up with lousy husbands. And the same thing happens in reverse."

"So you've resolved the problem by dropping out of it."

"I'm doing the best I can. Sometimes it doesn't seem like much." I signaled the waitress for two more drinks. "Let's talk about something else. You have a nice ass."

She looked startled for a second, but she didn't complain. I said, "You've also got great posture and excellent taste and a good mind. And if your husband won't get his nose out of *Wide World of Sports* and pay attention to you, he's lost his marbles. I'd love to go to bed with you."

She smiled at her glass, but she wouldn't look at me. "You know, I thought you were going to ask me. I hoped you would. But I thought you'd make it more romantic."

"If they had a violinist, I'd have him over here playing *Liebestod*. But it's just too damn much trouble to move that piano." The waitress plunked down our drinks and ambled away. I said, "I have shrimp and wine sauce at home that I think I can salvage from last night. We'll have cappuccino after dinner, and I'll put on my smoking jacket and seduce you properly."

"Do men really wear smoking jackets?"

"Gary Grant always seems to. Will you come?"

She looked at me steadily, measuring something. "I don't know. You're an attractive man, but I feel isolated from you. Or maybe by you. I don't think I'd really know you in a hundred years."

I didn't say anything. She said, "Besides, I have to fix dinner and drive a ten-year-old and an eleven-year-old to a roller-skating rink. Would you like to come along?"

"That's the best offer I've had all day, but I'll pass." We grinned at each other. A couple of real tough cookies.

We listened to the music while we finished our drinks. An old geezer with silver hair and a natty suit climbed up on one of the piano-bar stools and sat staring at his glass. He looked about eighty. I wondered what I'd be doing if I lived that long. I looked at Parker and Siehl, still talking up a storm. The mating dance of the storks. I said, "Who do you suppose is writing them."

Joan was in a reverie. She blinked and said, "Writing what?"

"The letters. Harrassing Parker."

"Oh, I don't know. If it isn't somebody who's crazy, it's probably someone who wants to run him out of town."

I said, "Oh, God, yes. *Especially*."

"Especially what?"

"There was something that bothered me about the letters, but I couldn't put my finger on it. Cathy Leeds finally made me see it. Whoever wrote the letters didn't use apostrophes, and the commas are in all the wrong places. But there are words like *especially* that pop up here and there. It feels like the writing of a smart person who's trying to sound dumb."

Joan said, "I don't know. Children don't write well, but they use surprising words once in a while."

"Maybe. It could be somebody who's a freak for *It Pays to Increase Your Word Power*. But I like your idea better. It's somebody who wants to run Parker out of town."

I realized that Joan had been staring at me for a

while. She said, "You never quit, do you?"

I said, "Twenty-four-hour service. We never sleep. Let's have another drink."

"No, I have to go."

"The shrimp dinner offer still stands."

"So does the roller skating."

We walked out past Parker and Siehl, past the old ladies in the lobby, and out into the parking lot. It was dark, and it was getting cold and windy. Joan walked to a blue Karmann-Ghia and unlocked the door. She began to get in when I said, "Wait." She stood up a little stiffly and looked at me. I touched her cheeks with my fingertips and leaned over and kissed her. Her mouth was like a warm cushion, and she touched my tongue tentatively with hers.

We looked at each other for a while. Then she said *Good night* in a voice that sounded tiny and unfamiliar. She got in her car, and I watched while she drove away.

It was a few minutes after six. I got in my car and sat there, I could still feel the hollows of Joan's cheeks in my fingertips. I wanted her fiercely.

My stomach started to growl, and I wondered what state of decay I'd find the shrimp in. I forced myself to think about Parker and the letters. Maybe Joan was right. I'd have to start nosing around the medical staff to find out who was the heir-apparent.

I decided to swing by the office to check the mail. The rush-hour traffic had subsided, and Central Parkway was deserted as a church on Saturday night.

The Kroger Building looked ugly and plasticky in the half-light. I pulled into the street-level parking garage entrance. It was dark as hell. Somebody had unscrewed two-thirds of the light bulbs in a fit of energy-conservation, and it looked like a stage lit for Jimmy Durante to make an exit. *Good night, Mrs. Calabash, wherever you are.*

I got out and locked the Impala. I was putting the key-case in my pocket when a voice said, "Nice car, Chief."

I couldn't see him in the gloom. I said, "You owe me two thousand dollars, Eddie."

"You, know, when a guy gets his tailbone broke, it's a real bitch to get around."

"You ought to know. You're the asshole expert."

He stepped into the light. He was wearing a fancy denim leisure suit under his leather coat. He had the magnum out, but it looked small in his hand. He said, "Smart mouth. You got one smart fucking mouth."

"All the cops think so, too. What brings you around?"

He moved up close so that his chest was touching mine and the gun poked into my abdomen. His breath stank. "You got no business to run your smart mouth at Korte."

"Korte likes to know when his boys get out of line. Especially on this side of the river."

"Yeah, he tol' me about that, smart-mouth prick." He shoved at my abdomen with the barrel of the gun.

I said, "Don't be stupid. If you screw up Korte's deal with the people over here, he'll make swiss cheese out of you and dump you down in the hills."

"That's why we ain't doin' nothin' over here. We're takin' a ride to Kentucky, Chief. You and me."

"You're dumber than you look. You keep up these independent operations and…"

Eddie shoved me back against the car. He was strong as an ox, but jittery. I didn't want that gun to go off. He said, "Shut up or I'll shoot you in the balls. Now, open the door and gimme the key."

I fished out the key-case with elaborate caution and unlocked the driver's door. I held out the keys to Eddie. He grabbed them out of my hand and strode around to the passenger's side. I fought off an impulse to duck down and try to scuttle away. With the magnum, he could shoot through the Impala and another car too.

Eddie climbed into the passenger's seat and said, "Get in, Chief. You're drivin'."

"Better think about this. You've got a long career in breaking arms…"

"Get in, cocksucker."

I got in, clipped the seat belt together, and started the car. Eddie sat angled around with his back to the passenger door. His gun was in his right hand, pointed at my liver. He rested his left arm on the back of the seat. His seat belt lay unlatched on the seat under his leg. I said, "Where to, Edward?"

He whipped around and glared at me. "Newport."

I eased the car out of the garage and headed south on Vine Street. I said, "You know your safety's on?"

"The fuck it is."

"Yeah, the safety's on, and you've got it all wiped clean, but it'll rust if you don't get some bluing on it. I guess some guys think revolvers are sexy, but I never thought..."

"Shut the fuck up." He kept glancing down to see if the safety *was* on. I said, "Your accuracy isn't worth a damn with that thing, compared to a pistol. It's probably zeroed at fifty yards, but beyond that..."

A pair of headlights loomed in front of us. Eddie looked up and yelled something about a one-way street. I yanked the steering wheel to the left and stood on the accelerator. We smashed into a parked car. The gun went off with a roar, and there was a hot streak across my abdomen. I lurched across the seat, grabbed the gun with my left hand, and back-fisted him twice with my right. He punched wildly with his left, grazing the side of my head and damn near tearing my ear off. I poked two fingers in his eyes, and he grabbed at his face with his left hand.

I pushed down on the magnum. He fired again and blew a hole in the floor. My ears started to ring. I couldn't break his grip on the gun. I jammed my right hand inside my coat and clawed at the shoulder-holster until I got the Browning loose. I pulled it out and cracked him on the temple with the butt. He sagged.

I pulled the magnum away from his limp fingers

and emptied the shells onto the floor. Eddie moaned and fumbled at his face. Outside in the street a circle of people were gathering, wide-eyed and scared. A flashing red light was playing over the faces of the crowd. I slipped the Browning and the magnum into my coat pockets and yanked at the door handle. It didn't make any noise. I was deaf.

I fought back a wave of nauseated panic and stepped out of the car. Something poked me in the ribs from behind, and I whirled around. It was a policeman with a gun. He was saying something that I couldn't make out. I said *I-can't-hear-you* in an exaggerated way, with no idea how loud I might be. Another cop moved in behind me and jerked my arms up. A sharp pain shot across my stomach, and I looked down at my coat. There was a powder-burn and a bullet-hole on the right side, and another tear on the left. There was a hole in the door of the car, too. My stomach felt wet, and I knew I was bleeding.

The cops pulled Eddie out of the other side of the car. The front end of the Impala was a crumpled mess, and steam was rising from the innards. A bus that had tried to swerve out of the way was stopped in the middle of the street with a smashed headlight. The bus passengers looked like pale cadavers in the dim fluorescent light.

One of the cops took the guns out of my pockets and made me lean against the car. I was too weak to resist. He opened my coat to frisk me, saw the blood, and yelled something at his partner. Everything seemed dreamy and far-away. They hustled me into a squad car, and the crowd parted as they pushed their way through.

After a few blocks I could dimly hear the siren. We roared along Vine Street while other cars jammed on their brakes and pulled over and tried to get out of the way. We shot past the blurry neon of the hillbilly bars and the bums and the hookers and the pasty-looking fat women with six or seven kids in tow. We climbed the long hill out of the downtown basin, and I started picturing the last scene from *The Sun Also Rises*. A car going up a hill... Or was that from *Room at the Top?* One of the cops nudged me and asked something that I couldn't hear. I realized that I'd been talking to myself, and I concentrated on keeping my mouth shut.

They didn't take me to Riverview. We went to the big general hospital where we sat in an emergency room that was crowded with old black men and women, pregnant teenagers, greasy-looking poor whites, and a junkie who kept talking to himself. After a while I was taken into a back room and examined and disinfected and taped up. Eddie's shot had chewed a gash in the skin of my abdomen, but it hadn't hit any organs.

My hearing came back slowly. I could hear crying babies and the frightened sobs of a woman across the hall. I kept thinking about Joyce and Cathy and the man she suffocated and sent down to the morgue. I wondered how many they killed over here.

The rest of the night took forever. They hauled

me back downtown to police headquarters, refusing to stop at a chili parlor to let me pick up some coneys. I was hungry as a wolf. I was left to sit in a small dirty room for a while, and then a detective-sergeant named Berger came in to interrogate me. He looked sad and intelligent, and he affected an air of *gee-buddy-isn't-this-a-wierd-situation?* I told him that Eddie had tried to take me for a ride because I was investigating a friend of his. When I wouldn't tell him who Eddie's friend was, Berger looked sadder and sadder. We jawed for half an hour. Berger told me about how he really didn't want to be a cop, but he'd been pressured into it by his family. I still wouldn't tell him who Eddie's friend was.

Finally Oberding barged through the door. He was fidgety and impatient. "Berger, get your ass out of here." Berger looked at me with a cold contempt he hadn't shown before and stomped out. Oberding said, "I warned you, piss-ant. You can get locked up for suppressing evidence."

"Evidence of what?"

"Evidence of why the hell is one of Korte's boys after you?"

"Forget it, Lieutenant. Eddie was on his own. He'd been warned to keep his tail out of here. You'll do him a favor if you lock him up, because Korte is going to take a dim view of him shooting up the neighborhood."

"You think you got all the answers, don't you?" I didn't say anything. Oberding said, "Son of a bitch bastard."

"Who's Berger? Part-time Chaplain?"

"Aaah, he thinks he's a psychiatrist. Dumb shit."

We sat there while Oberding lit one of his Luckies. I said, "Lieutenant, Eddie was trying to impress his girlfriend. I talked to her about a case that I'm working on, and he jumped to conclusions."

"Chandler, you son of a bitch!" He stood up and leaned over me, spraying spit and cigarette smoke. "We pull your ass out from under a city bus full of people who are all banged-up and bloody, and you and this torpedo are shooting the shit out of each other on the busiest street in town, and now you tell me it's because he jumped to goddamned *conclusions?*

"I told you that I'd share..."

"You want to *share* something, you bastard? There's a woman up in the hospital right now and they're trying to dig concrete splinters out of her face. She'll lose an *eye* because two shit-heads think they're above the fucking *law.*"

I felt drained and hollow. Oberding wasn't just mad. He was sick to death of me and all the other four-flushers who dumped their ugly messes on his doorstep.

"What do you want me to do, Lieutenant?"

"Go fuck yourself." He stared into space for a minute, breathing loudly through his nose. He said, "Don't let me catch you back in here, or I swear to God you'll never get out," and he left.

I was taken upstairs to an office full of detectives where I finally got a cup of coffee. They looked at my license and gun permit, and they ran a computer-check on my past sins. I gave them a detailed statement about Eddie's appearance at my office, about the cracked engine block in the Fairlane, and about what happened in the car on Vine Street. They kept asking me why Eddie was threatening me, and I kept telling them that they'd have to ask him.

There were delays and muttered conferences out of earshot and repetitious questions and all of the other things that the cops use to try to irritate you into changing your story. At eleven o'clock someone turned on a small portable television to watch the news. The top story was something political. The second story was about a wreck between a private vehicle and a Metro bus. There were "...indications of a gangland-style shoot-out involved in the incident, as well. Police are investigating."

At midnight they told me I was free to go, but not to leave town. When I tried to put on my coat, my taped-up stomach twisted and hurt. One of the detectives helped me get my arms into the sleeves. I was ready to leave when they brought Eddie into the room. He had a bandage around his head and a patch over one eye. He yelled when he saw me. "You fucker! You tried to poke my eyes out!"

"I just touched them, Eddie."

The cops who were escorting him tensed up. Eddie was so mad he was almost incoherent. "Bastard! Cocksucker!"

I said, "You shouldn't make people fight for their lives, Eddie. They'll do almost anything." They marched him over to a chair and made him sit down. I walked down a flight of stairs and out into the cold night air to hail a cab.

Chapter 10

I didn't sleep worth a damn that night. My left hand had been burned when Eddie fired the second shot, and it throbbed. My right ear was too sore to touch. The gouge in my belly hurt when I sat up in bed, and I knew there'd be no running for a while.

I cleaned up, fixed breakfast, and put the Browning back in the safe. I tried to call Parker. His office said that he was making rounds at Riverview. I called a cab and eased into a raincoat. My car-coat was sprawled on the couch like the carcass of a shot animal.

I got to Riverview at ten. Joan's desk was vacant, and her coat wasn't on the coatrack. Sisyphus peeked out from behind a tangle of hangers. I knocked on the door-frame, and Siehl waved me in. He was on the phone. While he finished his call, I wrote him a check for four hundred dollars.

He hung up and said, "Jesus Christ. Do you

know what happened last night?"

"I was there."

He looked incredulous. "You were?"

"Let's start over. What are you talking about."

"Parker's wife. And Darlene. Were you there?"

"No, I wasn't. What happened?"

Siehl shut the office door, and he came around the desk and sat with me in the circle of chairs. He said, "You know Parker's wife?"

"I've never met her."

"Well, she was out at Beechmont Mall last night, you know, shopping. And Darlene and that LPN she hangs around with were out there, too. Well, Parker's wife saw her, and I guess she knew who she was. So she walked up to Darlene and slugged her."

"I'll be damned. Did she hurt her?"

"Well, she knocked Darlene on her ass. Then one of the store managers, some woman, took Parker's wife aside and talked to her and got her to calm down. Then they called her daughter, and she came out to the mall and drove her home."

"What happened to Darlene?"

"Well, she's the problem, see. She wants to sue Parker's wife for assault and battery. Jesus!" He reached for a cigarette.

I said, "Darlene's got more guts than I thought."

"Are you kidding? Do you know what this is going to do to Dick Parker?"

I looked at Siehl sitting in his expensive chair, wearing his three-hundred-dollar suit. I thought about Parker and his *Children's Residence* phone. I said, "Maybe it'll teach him the difference between girls and women."

Siehl looked at me darkly. "What the hell does that mean?"

"I mean the next time Parker wants to dip his wick, he ought to pick on somebody his own size." I had a headache, and I hurt in three different places. I tore the check out of my checkbook and handed it to Siehl. "This makes us square. The next time you decide to have a vendetta with George Gibbs, leave me the hell out of it."

Siehl glowered at the check. I still felt mean as a snake. I said, "Is it worth it?"

"Is what worth it?"

"You make plenty of money. You've got more brains and education and power than most people ever dream of. You've got half of this hospital eating out of the palm of your hand. But you spend your time backstabbing one old fart and running circles around another. What's the point?"

"Who the hell do you think you are?"

"You've bought my time and you've got my silence as far as Parker's love-letters are concerned. But I'd be damn curious to talk to Gibbs and see if anybody around here ever worries about the patients. Or even sees them."

Siehl shot up out of his chair and moved in close, like Eddie had. The muscles on his neck all stood out, and his face was beet red. "Listen to me, you son of a bitch. You say one word to that old faggot and I'll have your goddamn license. You hear me, you bastard?"

And there it was. I said, "Are you serious?"

"You bet your sweet ass I am."

"I mean about Gibbs."

Siehl glared at me, but he didn't say anything. We fumed at each other like two bulls in a ring. I finally said, "I didn't ask you if *you* were queer. I asked you if Gibbs is."

"Hell, yes, he is! What the fuck are you implying?"

I looked at him and his fancy office again. It was like looking through the wrong end of a telescope. I said, "Good luck, Siehl. I wouldn't want to be on your goddamned merry-go-round for anything." I turned around while he was still fuming and walked out.

I started for the cafeteria to use one of the wall-phones, but I climbed the stairs to the second floor instead. Barry's office was still unlocked. I closed the door, sat at the desk, and doodled on a yellow pad until I calmed down and got the pieces to fit together.

I called the operator and paged Richard Parker. Another yellow sheet was filled with doodles before he called back. I told him that I had to talk to him immediately, but he said he'd be on rounds for another half an hour. I rummaged through Barry's desk. Besides the antihistamine inhaler, there were antacid tablets, eye drops, and dental floss. There was a full, orderly drawer of office supplies – index cards, paper clips, file folder labels, and boxes of colored marking pens. In the file drawer there were notes on disposable equipment, on medical records, and on job-enrichment projects in different hospitals. Tucked away in the back of a bottom drawer were paperback copies of *I'm OK – You're OK* and *The Prophet*. I wondered what kind of administrator he would have made.

Parker came into Barry's office looking like a mugging victim. His eyes were bloodshot, and he seemed to have shrunk inside his skin. He was wearing a white lab-coat. It was the first time he'd looked like a doctor instead of a middle-aged Lothario. He said, "What do you have to tell me?"

"I think I know who's been harassing you. But I need to know something from you first."

He sat down and touched the bridge of his nose with his thumb and forefinger. He looked ready to fall asleep. "What do you want?"

I said, "You've been a physician for a long time. You've had people climbing your frame since the first day you went into practice. You've been cussed and threatened and probably sued a few tines. But you got upset about some weepy little letters that accused you of having a sex life. Why?"

"For God's sake, Chandler, we discussed this before. I didn't concern myself about the letters until the telephone calls began."

"That still doesn't make enough sense. You could have changed your number or hired an answering service. You let yourself and your family become victimized too easily. What's behind all this?"

Parker breathed loudly but didn't say anything. I got impatient and said, "You told me that this had happened to you before, in Philadelphia. Is there any..."

"She killed herself."

We sat in the stuffy little office for several minutes without saying anything. I thought about Barry's eye drops and books. Parker grimaced and rubbed his hand across his forehead. Finally he said, "I broke off our affair. But then she had intense bouts of depression. I gave her medication, but she wouldn't take it. She almost never slept."

I tried to channel his drift. "So she wrote letters and made phone calls..."

"She finally took an overdose of Seconal. But she wrote a letter to my wife before she died, and she left a note as well. I've always believed that she felt that she would be saved, and that I would be forced to get a divorce and marry her. But she died."

"Was this common knowledge?"

Parker shook his head. "The police report was held in confidence. Of course, my wife got the letter."

We looked at each other for a while. I said, "So you got caught with your pants down, and you moved out of town to avoid a scandal. But that was ten years ago. What happened this time?"

"I don't appreciate your attitude, Chandler."

"If you'd told me about this last Monday, I wouldn't have to drag it out of you now,"

He glared at me, but it didn't last. He looked down and breathed loudly through his nose. "I wasn't terribly surprised when the letters began to come. I've seen too many other cycles of human behavior repeat themselves... Do you know what I mean, Chandler?"

"I think I do."

"When the telephone calls began, my wife became hysterical. Our relationship has always been a difficult one, and..." He paused. I didn't say anything. He said, "I've learned that she has had me followed. She has paid someone to compile a full report on my activities for the past three weeks." He looked at me with contempt. "One of your competitors, I assume."

"I don't compete on that level. When did you learn about this?"

"Last night. After..." He hesitated.

"After your wife took a swing at Darlene."

He nodded, sadly. "Darlene told my wife that she's going to sue her for assault. And so this morning my wife is seeing a lawyer about counter-suing for alienation of affection, or whatever grounds they can construct." He cradled his head in his hands. It had been a long night for the Parkers. He looked up at me suddenly. "Are you saying that Darlene wrote those letters?"

"No. It was someone who was waging a subtler war of nerves to run you out of town again."

"Who, for God's sake?"

"George Gibbs."

Parker looked at me as if I'd lost my mind. "Why on earth should George Gibbs..."

"Because you and Siehl were getting ready to de-throne Ross. The medical staff thinks he's a boob, and you were going to get rid of him and put Siehl in his place. Gibbs knew that he wouldn't last long under that arrangement. He couldn't get rid of Siehl, because he's built too strong a web of connections and obligations around here. So he decided to go after you. He dug out the facts about your dead girlfriend in Philadelphia, and then he started making it look like the same thing would happen here."

Parker looked at me suspiciously. "I just now told you about Lorraine – in Philadelphia. You make it sound as though you already knew about her."

"I assumed that you left Philadelphia under a cloud. You just filled in the details."

Parker stood up and paced around the room. He looked like a tired old man and nothing like a boudoir menace. He said, "Do you have a shred of evidence for any of this?"

"It's the only explanation that makes any sense of Barry Alspach's suicide."

"In what way?"

"Gibbs wasn't only Barry's Preceptor. He was screwing Barry, too."

Parker looked thunderstruck. "Oh, for the love of God," He fumbled in his coat pockets and came up with a pack of cigarettes. He sat down, lit one, and puffed on it without looking at me. After several minutes he said, "Have you established anything concrete? Have you examined his typewriter?"

"No, I haven't. That typewriter is probably at the bottom of the city dump by now. Gibbs probably got rid of it after Barry killed himself."

Parker said, "Christ Almighty," and kept smoking in silence. The ash fell off his cigarette and rolled down his lab-coat, making a tiny smudge. He said, "You realize, of course, that this says more about you than about George Gibbs."

"What do you mean?"

"I treat people every day who are trying to find someone to blame for everything. Some decide that it's the Communists. Others get angry about Big Business. Perhaps for you it's the homosexuals."

"I'm not talking about homosexuals. I'm talking about a vicious, stupid bastard who happens to be homosexual. Hell, homosexuals aren't any worse than anybody else. Or any better."

Out in the hall a cart with a squeaky wheel went rolling by. Parker's adrenalin began to wane, and he looked more and more wary as we sat there. Finally he said, "The sad truth is that it doesn't really matter."

"How's that?"

"I don't know that I entirely believe you. I detest George Gibbs personally, but I cannot accept the idea that he would do this thing."

"You don't have to. We can go to the police with the letters and a detailed explanation of what's happened. They'll take it from there. And they're persistent."

Parker shook his head again. "No. I am in an impossible situation. I cannot afford to have any legal actions taken by my wife or by – by Darlene. It's already far too public. I'm planning to move."

"You're serious?"

"It will take some time to close out my practice,

but yes, I am planning it. I don't feel that I have any choice."

Outside some raindrops began to splatter on the office window. I said, "Doctor, what about Barry Alspach?"

"What about him?"

"He's dead because of this business."

Parker stared at me a moment before answering. "I scarcely knew him. He must have been a very weak and unfortunate young man. I had patients who died the same day that he did. There was no justice in their deaths, either."

I looked out the window. It was going to be a dreary, drizzly day. I said, "You hired me on Wednesday, and you sent a five hundred dollar retainer. Today is Friday. That means..."

"Keep it, Chandler. You've earned it. As far as I'm concerned, this business is finished. I don't ever expect to see or hear from you again." He walked out and closed the door behind him.

I listened to the rain splatter and blow. I rubbed my belly and flinched when I pushed too hard on the bandage. It felt damp, and I looked in Barry's center desk drawer for Kleenex. On one of the three-by-five cards there was a scribbled list that included *paper towels* and *beer* and *Hamburger Helper*. And now he was laid out in a funeral parlor somewhere in New York. *There was no justice in their deaths, either.* Not unless someone decided to do something about it.

I left Barry's office and walked back downstairs to the administrative suite. Siehl wasn't in his office.

There was still no trace of Joan. I scribbled a note asking Siehl to call me, and I left it on his desk. I went back into the hall and walked to the far end where a double door was marked *Administrator.*

The secretary's office was bigger than Barry's. A fiftyish woman behind the desk sat ramrod-straight at the typewriter, wearing a black plastic earphone with wires that drooped down under the desk. She ignored me for a while. When she got around to looking at me, she had the eyes of an executioner. She said, "What do you want?"

"I need to talk to Mr. Ross."

"Concerning what?"

"Concerning Barry Alspach's suicide."

She looked at me like a fly on the cheesecake. "Mr. Ross spoke with Lieutenant Oberding last Tuesday. He's extremely busy at this time."

She waited for me to excuse myself. I waited for her to clamp a rose in her teeth and dance on the desk. Neither of us got anywhere. She was winding up for a firmer brush-off when I said, "Ross can either talk to me now or to the Homicide Squad this afternoon."

"He has *already spoken* to the police."

"This time we'll have the police and the reporters. You know how it is. They're all trying to be Woodward and Bernstein." She glared at me. I said, "It's up to you."

She charged up and out from behind her desk, and for a second I thought she was going to try to throw me bodily into the hall. She stormed through a connecting door into the next room and slammed it behind her. I looked at the magazine. It was an old copy of *Forbes*. There were other printed pieces on the end-table. One was a newsletter put out by a sterilizer company to advise hospital administrators on how to invest their money. There was also a four-color brochure titled *Riverview Hospital – Today and Tomorrow*. It was full of sexy, dramatic pictures and very little copy. It made Riverview look like the Baghdad Hilton.

The secretary emerged through the doorway and said, "This way." She sounded like Barton MacLane sending Cagney to the chair. I gave her my most winning smile, but it had about as much effect as a gnat flying into a brick wall. I stepped past her and into Ross's office.

It was a huge room. There were windows in two walls, with a bunch of framed sheepskins and certificates hanging between them. Ross had even framed his Flying Colonel certificate from United Airlines. He was sitting behind his desk, but it didn't look like he'd been working there. There was a flipchart on an easel with some magic markers in the tray. The heading on the flipchart was:

CODES FOR ROLES PLAYED
IN CARRYING OUT FUNCTIONS

Underneath there was a long list that included:

$P = primary$
$P^z = primary, specific$

$A = advisory$

$A^2 = advisory, specific$

$A_v = advisory, voluntary$

It went on and on. I couldn't make a lick of sense out of it.

I walked to his desk and said, "My name is Chandler. I appreciate..."

He said, "Pleased to meet you, Mr. Chandler," and he smiled. I was surprised until I looked into his eyes. He was a frightened, edgy man. The smile didn't mean a thing.

I sat in one of his conference chairs and said, "Mr. Ross, I have some information on the activities of one of your staff members. He's been harassing your Chief of Staff, and he was involved in precipitating Barry Alspach's suicide."

"My goodness!" He sounded as solicitous as a funeral director.

"He's a vicious creep and shouldn't be running around loose. I'm building a case against him which I'm going to turn over to the police as soon as I get hard evidence. That's why I've come to you."

"Me! Why?" He looked alarmed.

"You have the original copies of the poison-pen letters that were written to Richard Parker. I need them. When other samples from the same typewriter are identified, a case can be made in court."

"You've seen the letters?"

"I've seen copies. They're shaky as evidence. With the originals, the police lab can match paper fibers and ink samples."

Ross sunk his chin into his chest like a ham actor playing Clarence Darrow. "You haven't told me who this staff member is."

"I can't. There's a possibility that I'm completely wrong, and that the guilty party has nothing to do with your hospital. But I doubt it. I know who it is, and I need those letters to establish positive proof."

Ross began to shake his head while staring at his desk. "I feel these are delicate matters, Mr. Chandler." I didn't say anything. He said, "I feel that if Dr. Parker wanted to have these letters investigated, he would have arranged it."

"He did. He gave them to you."

He said, "I'm sure that he gave them to me because he knew I would handle them in confidence, and that is what I'm going to do." He had a blurry voice that made all his words run together.

I said, "You gave copies to your executive staff. That's about as confidential as putting up a neon sign."

"You seem to know a lot about my affairs, Mr. Chandler. How do you come to know about these things?"

My stomach began to churn. "The people who hired me expect me to keep my mouth shut, and I'm going to. I can understand that you don't want to give the letters to me. Give them directly to the police."

"I don't feel that that's appropriate."

"Your Chief of Staff entrusted you to settle this mess."

"He has informed me that he will be moving soon, and that consequently he will no longer be able to serve as Chief of Staff,"

"Do you think your responsibility ends there?"

This time he put on his indignant look. "Are you presuming to tell me my responsibilities, Mr. Chandler?"

"Somebody has run your Chief of Staff out of town. Somebody has driven a nice conscientious kid to suicide. That person is in this building and on your payroll. I think that ought to demand some of your attention."

"I'm just trying to run a hospital, Mr. Chandler. I'm not interested in the personal lives of my employees."

"You smug bastard." Ross jumped and looked at me in horror. My stomach hurt, and my ear was throbbing. I said, "You self-seeking son of a bitch. You're glad Parker's leaving because he was getting ready to dump you. No wonder everybody in this hospital runs around covering their ass. That's all *you* do. You sit up in this throne room and dream up abbreviations for some goddamned textbook that nobody's ever going to read. You play your staff against each other so that nothing ever gets done. You're so goddamn out-of-touch with this place that patients are dying because you won't hire enough nurses." He was getting panicky and shooting desperate glances at the phone, but I didn't feel like stopping. "That's the trouble with god-damned organizations. They end up being led by schmucks like you or bastards like Richard Nixon."

He hit the intercom button, and his secretary came storming in through the door. I said, "I'll let myself out, thanks," and did.

Chapter 11

The rain had turned into a steady drizzle, with gusts that felt like cold slaps in the face. I took a cab to my office. The Christmas decorations in the store windows looked cheerless in the gray light. I hadn't thought about Christmas, and I didn't want to. Holidays weren't my good times.

I dried my hair with a paper towel from the men's john. When I lifted my arms, my stomach bandage twisted and hurt. That was all right. It kept me from having second thoughts.

I settled in at my desk, threw away most of the mail, and called Oberding at headquarters. A desk sergeant with a bored monotone told me that the Lieutenant was busy, but that he'd make sure that he got a message to call me back. I wondered what Oberding was doing. Probably eating lunch. I sat and fiddled and fumed for half an hour. Nobody called, not even the long-life light-bulb people.

I rang up the hippie restaurant, ordered a

sandwich, and tried to talk somebody into delivering it. No chance. I put my raincoat on and hustled down the block to pick it up. I got back and regretted that I hadn't also bought some coffee or juice. Their homemade bread was dry as cardboard.

I doodled and made lists and leafed through old magazines until the phone finally rang. Oberding didn't bother to introduce himself. "What is it, Chandler?" He sounded like his hemorrhoids were itching.

"Lieutenant, I told you I'd let you know if anything turned up about Barry Alspach."

"You told me that ten times already. You think I got a short memory? "

"I know what happened to Barry, but I need your help to prove it."

"I know what happened, too. He killed himself. We wrapped that one up two-three days ago."

"He was pushed into it."

Oberding snorted loudly over the phone. "What the hell does that mean?"

"Barry was working with an old queer at the hospital. The guy was screwing him." Oberding snorted again and said *Bah* to nobody in particular. I said, "Barry found out that the guy was writing poison-pen letters and pulling some other crap. They had a confrontation, and the guy threatened to expose Barry as a homosexual. So he killed himself."

All I could hear for fifteen seconds was Oberding's loud breathing. There was the click of a cigarette lighter, and some huffing and puffing as he got it going. Finally he said, "Chandler, where do you dream up this shit?"

"It's circumstantial, but a case can be made."

"For what?" I didn't say anything. Oberding said, "There ain't any case. Even if the guy cornholes the kid and then the kid kills himself, that don't lead to charges. The kid was over eighteen."

I switched the phone to my right hand, and it hurt when it banged against my sore ear. "Dammit, Lieutenant, you bust people for smoking grass and showing skin flicks and pissing in alleys. Here's a kid who's dead..."

"That shit's against the law." We fumed at each other in silence. Finally Oberding said, "You ain't given me anything to hang my hat on, anyway. Maybe you're right, maybe you're wrong. I can't move unless you got something to show me."

"Yeah. Right." My stomach began churning again. I said, "What did you do with Eddie, besides pound the piss out of him?"

"The guy that come in with you? Turned out there was a Federal warrant out for him. He was one of those guys that tried to bring a boatload of grass into New Orleans. Dumb shit."

I didn't know if he meant Eddie or me. I said, "Okay, Lieutenant. I delivered what I promised."

"Don't be a smartass, Chandler. Bring me something I don't have to draw a picture of."

"Right. I'll let you know when I find a bloodstained fingerprint."

Oberding said, "Yeah, do that," and he hung up.

I sat and listened to the rain splatter down the air-shaft. There was no joy in Mudville, for damn sure. No case, no crime, no problem. The smartest thing I could do would be to go home and sleep and let my belly heal.

Instead I put on my coat and got soaked walking two blocks to a low-budget rent-a-car franchise. The guy who ran the place looked like he stole his merchandise from a parking garage in Cleveland. I rented a Mustang. It smelled like somebody had peed in it, but I didn't care. I fired it up and drove to Riverview.

I passed by the visitors' parking lot entrance and circled the hospital. A web of service drives ran around the building from the main entrance to loading docks and small lots. There were signs that said *Keep Out* and *Official Business Only*. I followed the drive that led toward the Emergency Room. Just before the loop that ran under the ER canopy, a driveway branched off the service road and led to a medium-sized parking area.

I cruised the lot. Most of the cars had medical insignia on the bumpers. There were stencilled signs on short poles in front of each parking space. Three of them said *ROSS* and *SIEHL* and *GIBBS*. Gibbs's spot had a car in it. There was an empty slot three Cadillacs away that said *PARKER*. I eased the Mustang into the space, hoping that Parker wouldn't be back for the afternoon. If he did, to hell with him. I could have him change my bandage.

It was 3:30. I left the car and walked through

the rain to the Emergency Room entrance. The ER waiting room looked like a country-club lounge, and there was nobody in it. I wondered how things were going over at General with the junkies and the blacks and the old ladies. A nurse looked at me from behind a sheet of glass. I ignored her and walked on into a corridor that looked like it led into the hospital. She went back to whatever she was reading.

I found a room full of vending machines and bought three packs of cheese-crackers. I slopped back to the car through the shoe-deep water in the parking lot. Gibb's Monte Carlo was still there. The rain kept up a monotonous drone, and the windows started to fog over. I wondered where Siehl's car was. I tried listening to the radio, but it was god-awful. There was a leak at the top of the rear window, and water dripped onto the back seat. An hour crawled by like a cripple.

Gibbs finally came out. He hunched down under an umbrella and scurried across the parking lot. He ducked into his car, fiddled around for a minute, and then backed out of his parking space. I let him get around the corner of the building before I started the Mustang.

I caught up with him at the main entrance. He didn't seem to notice. He pulled out into traffic and wove through several residential streets before he emerged onto Reading Road. His back window was fogged over, and he wouldn't have known if a Mack truck was on his tail.

He turned into Eden Park and began to head

toward Mount Adams. For a few anxious blocks I wondered if he had spotted me and was going to lead me to my own front door. Instead he pulled into the parking lot of a restaurant in an expensive high-rise. I parked the Mustang down the block and watched while he sloshed across the street and into the building. I wondered if he lived there. I waited five minutes before following him.

Inside the high-rise lobby there were two snazzy-looking sixty-year-old women waiting for their car to be brought around. They looked like they were faring better than their sisters at the Vickers Hotel. I passed the locked doors that led to the apartment lobby and followed the corridor around to the restaurant.

Gibbs was sitting at the horseshoe bar. The place was full of well-dressed people going on their Friday-afternoon bender. It looked like a lawyer-stockbroker crowd, with expensive-looking women hanging on their elbows. A guitarist was playing 'Sixties folk music in the background. I sat on a stool two seats away from Gibbs. He was curled around a Manhattan and smiling to himself.

A bartender with a sculptured moustache eyed my clothes without being impressed and said, "What do you want?"

"Do you have Amaretto?"

"Yeah. You want a Godfather?"

"No... I think... I think I'll just have an Amaretto and soda."

He looked appalled and went away to fix it. The

guitarist launched into a cocktail-lounge version of *Blowin' in the Wind*, I tried not to look at Gibbs. The bartender brought back the drink in a wine glass and plunked it down on a napkin. "You want me to run a tab?"

"Would it... do you mind if I pay for them as I go along?"

He rolled his eyes in mock surrender and said, "Whatever you want, friend." I paid a dollar and a quarter and let another quarter clatter noisily onto the bar,

I could feel Gibbs checking me out, but I concentrated on diddling with my drink. It tasted like cream soda, I wondered if I was overdoing it. I was calculating how to break the ice with Gibbs when he said, "Excuse me."

"Yes?"

"Weren't you in my office last Tuesday afternoon?"

"Mr. Gibbs! I sure was. My name's Frank." I stuck out my hand.

He took it, but unenthusiastically. "If I remember correctly, your name is Chandler, and you're a detective."

"Well, I was trying to be." I took a deep breath and wondered how much Siehl had told Gibbs about why he'd hired me. I said, "I was a friend of Barry Alspach's. When he killed himself, I felt like I had to find out why."

"But David Siehl told me that you were working for him."

I took another deep breath and said, "I was. Mr. Siehl was suspicious that his... Well, I'm really not supposed to tell you. But he needed someone to do some watching for him, and Barry knew that I was out of work, and so he recommended me. So I worked for a few days for Mr. Siehl. And then when Barry... You know..." I let it trail off. I felt like a blithering idiot.

Gibbs took a pull at his drink and stared at it in mock concentration. He and Ross had taken lessons at the same school. He said, "What kind of work do you normally do?"

I said, "I used to teach English. Then they laid off a lot of us last year, and I haven't been able to find work since. And now I'm not working for Mr. Siehl any more, either."

"I know. No one is."

I felt a knot starting to form in my stomach. "I don't follow you."

"He was fired this afternoon."

I closed my eyes and listened to the drone of chatter in the bar. It was the insouciant prattle of careless people, insulated by money and alcohol from any real worries. Dylan's anthem, leached of its lyrics, wafted inconsequentially over the crowd like elevator music. I said, "What happened?"

Gibbs looked out across the lounge at the rain-soaked windows and the blurry view of downtown. He could barely conceal a grin. "He had been entrusted with copies of some confidential papers. Our Administrator asked to have them returned this afternoon, and David didn't have them. He was fired."

And so you're out celebrating, you old bastard. I said, "Oh, well," and looked at the bar napkin. I wondered who was playing games with whom.

A blonde woman asked if the seat between Gibbs and me was taken. I said, "Why don't you have this one?" and I moved next to Gibbs. He didn't seem to mind. He was still relishing Siehl's downfall. I sipped at my syrupy-tasting drink and waited.

Gibbs said, "It's very strange, you know."

"What is?"

"You were very forceful when you came to my office. You threatened to bring an investigative reporter unless I spoke with you. Now you seem almost hesitant. You seem like two different people." He looked me in the eye for the first time. "Which is the real you?"

"I wish I knew."

Gibbs didn't change expression. I thought *Forgive me, Barry* and said, "I was really upset when Barry killed himself. I hadn't known him long, but – I thought perhaps that someone had gotten him involved with drugs. I thought that it might have been some of the people he was working with at the hospital, and that was why I asked you what he was working on."

Very softly, Gibbs said, "Why did you come up here this afternoon?"

"I only live two blocks from here."

He said *Hmmmm* and rubbed his fingers up and down his glass. I stared at the bubbles in my

Amaretto. The bartender mixed a Singapore Sling with a lot of rattling and served it to the blonde woman with a flourish. I said, "Barry liked you, too."

Gibbs looked alarmed. "What did he say about me?"

"Just that he thought you were a good man to work for." The bartender eyed our glasses pointedly. I said, "Mr. Gibbs, may I buy you a drink?"

"With David Siehl's money?"

"Not really. It's my money now."

"Of course. Don't pay any attention to that last remark. I'll buy the drinks."

We got two more glasses of hooch, and Gibbs paid with a twenty. I decided to see where he would go with things. He drank most of his drink in silence. He looked like a pale reptile with thinning hair and pudgy lips and an out-of-shape body. I couldn't guess how old he was.

He stuck a finger into his glass and poked at the maraschino cherry. He said, "If your name is Chandler, you must be English."

"I don't know."

"Really? That's odd."

"I was adopted, Mr. Gibbs. My foster parents had a Balkan name that I never liked. So after they died, I decided to treat myself to a new name."

"Why did you pick Chandler?"

"It was the name of a writer I admire very much."

Gibbs said, "That's interesting. You're fortunate, you know."

"Why do you say that?"

"I think that most of us have a lot of hangups that we got from our parents. I guess you don't have any hangups – or do you?"

Gibbs was off and running. For the next three hours we sat and drank while he grilled my psyche. His questions were two-thirds insinuations, and he asked them with a familiar air that got more pronounced as he kept drinking. *Why did I like to read so much? Had I ever been married? Did I get lonely?* I rattled off soulful answers like a preppie on a first date while I drank enough Amaretto to dip a sheep.

I didn't have much luck getting Gibbs to talk about himself. He was married, had children, and lived on the west side of town. He was proud that he had a degree in sociology instead of administration. He didn't like being a hospital administrator, but he didn't have any choice this late in life. Nobody appreciated him because nobody understood him. I nodded sympathetically and tried to get him to go on, but he liked to lead the conversation too much to give up the interlocutor's role for long.

The dinner hour slid by unnoticed. Gibbs had a bottomless capacity for liquor. My stomach was churning with all the sweet glop I was pouring down. Flirting with men wasn't a damn bit easier than flirting with women.

By nine o'clock Gibbs was beginning to blur his words. I was in the middle of a long trite soliliquy about how Europeans were more sensitive and humane than Americans when he interrupted me and said, "Y'know, you're an inneresting person. You don't meet very many these days."

"Thanks, George. I take that as quite a compliment."

He looked woebegone. "I don't find many people that I can really talk to."

"Me neither. You know what might be interesting?"

"What's that?"

"How'd you like to smoke some grass?"

He shrugged. "Y'know, I've smoked before."

"Sure. Everybody has. I just thought it might be kind of a friendly thing to do tonight. Don't you think so?"

"Oh, it might be. Is that the sort of thing you like?"

"I certainly do. And I've got some terrific Colombian." Gibbs hesitated and looked me over. I said, "Come on. This place is a drag."

"C'mon where?"

"I told you. I just live around the corner from here."

I stood up. Gibbs said, "Jesus, you're tall."

"Come on. Let's kick up our heels a little."

We bumbled to the coat-check and made jokes about how all tan raincoats look alike. Outside the drizzle continued steadily. Gibbs started for his car, but I rhapsodized about how much fun it was to walk in the rain. We shared the umbrella for the two blocks to my apartment, bumping into each other as much as possible.

We stumbled inside, and Gibbs plopped down on the couch and started mopping his ears and neck with Kleenex. I launched into a routine about how I'd always wanted to fix the place up while I got out a bottle of brandy. We toasted all the misunderstood people in the world.

Gibbs said, "Where's your television set?"

"I don't have one. I see too much of the outside world already. How do you like the brandy?"

"Hmmm. Five Star. Nice."

"Wait till you see the grass." I went into the kitchen and got out the corncob pipe and the sandwich-bag with the ounce of dope in it. I switched the radio on to the University's classical-music station and plunked down beside Gibbs on the couch. He looked at the pipe and said, "Douglas MacArthur." I grinned and said, "I shall return."

I puffed on the pipe to get it started and passed it to Gibbs. He inhaled a good lungful. I held the smoke in my mouth and tried to let it out when he wasn't looking. The ritual of smoking and breath-holding and passing the pipe eliminated the need for conversation, and I was grateful. I was running out of cute things to say.

We finished the pipe and Gibbs sagged back with a big sigh. "Ooooh. That's nice stuff, Frank."

I was feeling a slight buzz. "Yep."

He giggled. "All of a sudden I'm thirsty."

"That's too goddamned bad."

He grinned at first until he saw that I wasn't

kidding. He started to look frightened, but then he began to smirk. "Mmmmm. So you're a rough one, eh?"

"Not by choice." I stood up, shut off the music, and turned on every light in the place. Gibbs didn't move. I dragged a kitchen chair into the living room and sat down in front of him, knees to knees. He sank back in the couch. His breath stank with the grass. I said, "Okay. What happened with Barry?"

"What do you mean?" He made little fists, with his thumbs tucked inside.

"Don't be cute. I want to know what you did, and what he did."

"Are you going to hit me?"

"No. I think you'd like that too much. I've got something more permanent in mind."

Gibbs whimpered while his stoned imagination worked overtime. I said, "If you want to walk out of here, you'd better start talking about last Monday night."

"Monday?" He looked dazed. He was having a hard time remembering.

"Okay. Forget Monday. Tell me about Richard Parker and David Siehl."

He began to splutter. Now his mental dial was set on *mad*. "Those bastards. It wasn't fair."

"What wasn't fair?"

"I've been an administrator for twenty years. Those bastards were going to... I helped *interview* David Siehl. They were trying to get rid of me."

"So you decided to get rid of them."

Now Gibbs was shaking his head theatrically, like Ross. "They had no right. It wasn't fair. They both had plenty of skeletons in their closets, let me tell you."

"Like what?"

"Richard Parker drove some poor girl to suicide." He tried to look indignant, but he didn't have enough chin to carry it off.

"So you wrote letters to tell Parker what you thought of him."

"It wasn't just me."

"Oh?"

He began to sound like Ida Lupino. "I hear people talking about him all the time."

"You're no angel yourself. You were having a thing with Barry Alspach."

"Barry was an adult." Clifton Webb.

"You were supposed to teach him, not fuck him. What happened on Monday night?"

He started to glance around wildly, and he put his hands over his mouth. I knocked his hands away, and he banged his head back against the wall. "Did you go over to Barry's apartment on Monday night?" He started to cry. I slapped him across the face. "Did you?"

"Yes. Don't hit me."

"What did Barry tell you?" He grimaced and bit his lip. I smacked him again. "Goddamnit, I'll break your nose."

"He called me on the phone. He *asked* me to come over."

"Lucky you. So you went over..."

"And he – I – he said that he saw the letters."

I leaned back to give him a little breathing space. "And?"

"And – he asked me if I wrote them. But he already knew."

"And what did you do?"

He said *Oh!* and tried to push me away. He shoved at my stomach and tore the bandage loose. The pain shot everywhere. I knocked his hands away and punched him in the chest. He started to double over, but I jammed his shoulders back against the couch. "One more time. What did you do?"

"I told him..."

"You told him what?"

"I told him that I'd report him. To his school."

"For what?"

"For sexual misconduct."

I pushed Gibbs away and stood up and stormed around the room. "You miserable prick. You cold-hearted cocksucker. Is there anything you won't do?"

"I didn't think..."

"You didn't think what?"

He was gasping like a drowning man. "You don't know what it's like! I'm... I can't... My wife despises me..."

"I wonder why."

"...I get so damned lonely that I drive down to the bus station..."

"Is that before or after you call Parker's house and drive his wife crazy? Or bully a kid that you're supposed to be teaching?"

I stopped pacing. Gibbs said, "Don't hit me any more. Please."

"Shit. That'd be letting you off too easy." Gibbs looked at me like a wounded animal. I said, "Don't worry. I wouldn't touch you with rubber gloves. But I'm going to do what you did."

"What?"

"I'm going to write letters," He stared, numb. I said, "I'm going to write to your wife. Then I'll write to Ross and every member of the Riverview Board of Trustees."

"No. Please."

"And then there's the County Prosecutor and the State Attorney General. And the American Hospital Association. And the newspapers. The difference is that I'm going to sign them."

"Don't. I – no. Please don't."

"I'll mail them on Monday. I'll give you that long to clean up your own mess."

Gibbs was shaking and crying. This time it was real. He looked at me with blubbery defiance. "You bastard. You can't do this."

"Don't bet on it." I grabbed his arm and yanked him to his feet. I marched him to the door and threw his raincoat and umbrella out into the hall. "Get out. And get busy before Monday." I pushed him out and slammed the door behind him. I heard him stumbling around in the hall trying to get his coat on. A little later the downstairs door banged shut. Outside the wind gusted and splattered the windows with rain.

Chapter 12

Saturday I slept until noon. My impulse was to get up and barge around furiously, doing things and staying in motion. Instead I stayed in bed and forced myself to think through the business with Gibbs the night before. I felt dirty, but not sorry.

I got up and changed the dressing on my abdomen gingerly. There was going to be a fancy-looking scar that would ruin my career as a go-go dancer. I made eggs and toast and coffee. I called Siehl's home, but there was no answer. I tried to call Parker, but a snippy woman at the phone company told me that his number had been disconnected. I called his office. Another doctor was seeing Parker's patients, and nobody had any idea where he was.

I put on two sweaters under a raincoat and drove downtown to the open-air market. It was still raining lightly, and the stalls were swaddled with canvas. I bought peppers and tomatoes and eggs to make *huevos rancheros*. The market was a good place to be. It was full of people who had nothing more devious in mind than filling a shopping bag with fresh food. I poked around and looked in all the stalls and wrote down the number to order a poster of *Edible Molluscs and Crustaceans from* the U.S. Government Printing Office.

I came back to the apartment as tired and footsore as a fifty-year-old bureaucrat. I blamed it on my sore belly and lay down on the couch to rest my eyes for fifteen minutes. When I woke it was dark. I called Siehl's home, and again no one answered. The shrimp and wine sauce were still in the refrigerator. I whipped up a meal and wondered if I was poisoning myself.

After eating I went to the second-run movie theater in Mount Adams. They were showing *The Longest Yard*, Altman's *Images*, and, at midnight, *Fat City*. I let the movies carry me for six hours, and it was nearly two a.m. before it was over. I walked home and fell into a grateful dreamless sleep.

On Sunday morning there was a freezing rain that stuck to the windows. I lay in bed for a long time and listened to the church bells. The tones were muffled by the wind, and it sounded like a funeral. The sky was the color of lead. I couldn't find a way to give shape to the day. I stared at things and tried not to give in to the ugly gloom that was hovering within reach.

I dragged myself out of bed and drove to a restaurant for breakfast. It was a plastic-and-stainless-steel place where coffee cost thirty cents a cup. I sat at the counter and scowled. There were families and kids and clusters of old ladies on their way home from church. There were sweethearts and young couples who had just crawled out of bed. Two seats down the counter there was a crazy old man who kept muttering over his coffee. He was talking to himself and hoping desperately that somebody would hear him. I wondered if I'd end up that way. Outside the sleet hammered down steadily.

The afternoon lasted forever. I dug out an old copy of *All The King's Men* and tried to read it again, but it was just ink on pieces of paper. When Anne Stanton appeared, I started thinking of Joan. I wanted to bring her over and hold her close and chase away the chill with brandy and coffee. Memories of rubbing elbows with Gibbs came back in an unwelcome flash. I wanted Joan. I wanted a woman in my life.

Afternoon darkened into evening. I napped again and woke fiercely hungry. I drove to a restaurant near the university where they had dim lights and fancy cheeseburgers with bearnaise sauce and good-looking coed waitresses. I munched and sipped beer and tried to remember the name of the actress who had played the alcoholic girlfriend in *Fat City*.

I felt better in the restaurant, but the gloom and the quietness were waiting when I got back to the apartment. I tried to read again, but I gave up in near-despair. It was too quiet. The apartment looked shabby and empty. When I was a kid, Sunday nights had meant Ed Sullivan and *Alfred Hitchcock Presents*. A television could help, but it would still be lonely to watch.

I took two aspirin and drank half a glass of Scotch. I put a Chopin album on the scratchy old stereo in the bedroom. I turned down the volume, got under the covers, and read until I fell asleep.

The phone woke me on Monday morning. It was still connected to the recorded-answer gadget, but I got it before the machine could start its spiel. My voice was still hoarse with sleep. "Hello?"

"Frank? Oh, thank God you're there. Everything over here is just awful."

"Where are you?"

"I'm at the hospital. I came in today, and Mr. Siehl's been fired, and ..."

"I know. Is he gone already?"

"His desk is empty, and all of his things are gone. I guess he came in over the weekend and took everything."

"Where were you on Friday?"

"Oh, I was home with the boys. Paul was sick... Listen, that's not the important thing. Did you hear about Mr. Gibbs?"

I took a deep breath and said, "No."

"He was killed last night. He started his car inside his garage and – and the fumes killed him."

You don't know what it's like... My wife despises me...

"...everybody here is wondering whether or not it was suicide," she was saying. "All anybody can talk about is his insurance money..."

He must have been a weak and unfortunate young man... There was no justice in their deaths, either...

"...God, people can be awful..."

What the hell did you expect?

"Frank! What are you saying?"

I snapped out of it. "What did I say?"

"It sounded like you were asking me what — what I expected."

"Sorry if I said anything crass. I lost it there for a minute. That's too bad about Gibbs. Did he have children?"

"I don't think — no, I'm not sure..."

She sounded shaken and unhappy. We let a few seconds go by in silence. I said, "Joan?"

"Yes?"

"Does anybody know where Siehl has gone?"

"I heard Mr. Ross's secretary say that he had already found another job in Atlanta. He must have been talking with them before."

"It sounds like Siehl to have an escape hatch. Is that picture of Sisyphus still there?"

"The what?"

"The one behind the coatrack."

"Do you mean — yes, it is."

I said, "Joan, I want to ask you to do something. Do you have any reason to stay over there?"

"No. I — they're talking about reassigning me,

but I just want to get out of this place."

"Good. Take down that picture and bring it over here."

"What? Why..."

"I'll make the effort to see that it gets back to Siehl. If you leave it there, somebody will just throw it out. And if he doesn't want it, I'd like to have it." She didn't say anything. I could hear her breathing. I said, "Oh, hell, forget the picture. Please come over. You've got the whole day free. We can sit here and drink coffee and talk about this business. I may try to seduce you, but I won't lock you in."

"Silly. That sounds nice, but..."

"But what?"

"It frightens me, Frank. You frighten me. I like you, and I'm attracted to you – but as much as I want to know you, I'm afraid that you'll be nothing but hurt for me. You're a spooky man, you know."

"I don't see why. I keep peculiar hours, and I yell at people sometimes, but compared with those vacant souls you work with, I've got to be an improvement."

"I don't know how to explain it. The funny part is that I decided to leave Bill this weekend. I wouldn't even have anything to feel guilty about. But I'm just not sure I'm ready for you right now."

I listened to the silence in the apartment. "I can't say that I blame you. Life is full of lousy choices."

We said goodbye and hung up. I went into the kitchen and put the teakettle on the stove. I could feel the grit on the floor underfoot. Gloomy men and twice-shy women had no business together, anyway. *Que sera, sera*, and to hell with it. Outside it had started to snow big, wet flakes that wouldn't stick. It was supposed to be a cold winter. Dandy. It would suit my mood just fine.

The kettle shrilled, and I made coffee. I sat at the table, wiped some old toast-crumbs away and looked out the window. I could see a dim reflection in the glass. The table and chairs and I were suspended like ghosts over the river valley. I felt like a ghost. I felt like a disembodied spirit who didn't fit in this world or any other. If you were a ghost, you could rattle your chains and point to the scene of the crime. But if nobody believed in you, you weren't really there.

I finished the coffee and got up. There was no one to hold or cherish. The second best medicine was sleep. I walked slowly back into the bedroom, hoping, but not really believing, that I'd hear a knock at the door.

About the Author

Tom Sigafoos writes novels, short stories, travel articles, mystery parties, and workshop guides for counselors and teachers. His work has appeared in *AMERICA'S HQRSE*, the magazine of The American Quarter Horse Association, in *Ireland's Horse & Pony* magazine, and in *Creative Holidays* Travel Magazine.

He has also worked as a business planner, marketing consultant, and technical writer. He served as Chair of the Corporate Member Council of the American Society for Engineering Education (ASEE) and as a member of the Steering Committee for the Center for Research in Engineering Education of the National Academy of Engineering (NAE).

Since 2003 he has lived in County Donegal, Ireland.

For additional information contact tomsigafoos@gmail.com